Hearts Off Course

OCTAVIA P. PRICE

Copyright

This book is a work of fiction. Any names, characters, companies, organizations, places, events, locales, and incidents are either used in a fictitious manner or are fictional. Any resemblance to an actual person, living or dead, or actual companies or organizations, or actual events is purely coincidental.

First Edition February 28,2026

Written by Octavia P. Price

ISBN: 979-8-9936155-1-6.

CHAPTER 1
Crystal Harris

"Mmm, that feels so good. Mmm, mmm, you really know how to make me feel good. Go deeper, yeah, that's it, right there. That's the spot! Mmmm, I could have you do this all day, every day. Oh yeah, ooo, yeah! Yeah!"

I closed my eyes and smiled. A feeling of relief and pleasure shot through my body.

"You always make me feel better."

Trey ran his large hands slowly up and down my back.

I didn't know if this was appropriate to say, but I love, I mean like, my massage therapist, Trey. I have been going to him ever since I came back to the states from my United Kingdom internship.

When I came back from the WCP London office, my heart was broken by Spencer, or should I say, Vice President Spencer Williams. Just thinking of him evoked a stabbing pain in my gut. I hoped that distance and time would help the pain go away from our broken relationship. I knew I never wanted to feel this hurt ever again. I wasn't just heartbroken, I was still angry for the way I was treated and the way the relationship ended.

My friend Chaundra encouraged me to get a massage. She was one of my besties from college, and she noticed that my spirits were low.

"Crystal, you need to move on, and one of the best ways to feel better is

by taking care of yourself. Get a massage, you will feel better and relieve stress."

Sitting at the local coffee shop, scrolling through social media, I gave all the happy couples on Facebook likes and hearts to their post. The posts just made me feel worse. I decided to take Chaundra's suggestion and get a massage. After scrolling through three pages, Trey's massage therapy stood out to me. He was very positive with his inspirational and encouraging words.

Love yourself with a massage today and start the healing.

Feeling eager and energetic, I called the number that was provided and made an appointment for the same day. I drove to the address and saw the sign, Body Unwind Now. I got out of my Lexus IS and walked up to the door. I knocked lightly, and fifteen seconds later, the door opened, and Trey appeared with a smile. He stood to the side and welcomed me into the studio.

I must say he wasn't bad to look at either, standing six feet tall, long pencil-sized locs swooped up in a tie. His smooth brown skin was accented with beautiful lips, ebony-colored eyes, and long eyelashes. His brilliant white smile made me feel warm, protected, and secure. In the middle of the room, I observed a table draped with white sheets. Low amber lighting illuminated the various green plants, creating a very peaceful scene.

"Welcome, Crystal. This is a safe place for you to let go of all your stress. Do not hold back your feelings. What I mean is, if you want to talk about your problems and get them out, do so. If you want to scream or cry, you can do that too. Again, this is a safe space. Now I am going to leave the room, and you can disrobe to your liking; you can take all your clothes off, or you can keep them on. I do ask that you take off your shoes. Once you are ready, get under the covers and call me to enter the room. I will be in my office," Trey finished with a smile.

I replied back, "Okay," with a smile of my own.

Trey left the room, and I was alone. I was so eager to get this massage, but now I was feeling shy. I was suddenly too shy to remove my clothes and allow this hot ass man to massage me. I had not had a male's hands on me in a year, not since Spencer touched me when we were in a relationship. I took a deep breath and began to take off my shoes, socks, pants, and blouse. I stood there in my bra and panties.

I sighed before attempting to give myself a pep talk.

"Well, I might as well take it all off. I need a new beginning. I can't be afraid. I need to be bold, not apprehensive, and insecure. Trey is a professional massage therapist, and he has seen several bodies unclothed. I need to stop being afraid."

I told myself.

I began to pull off my panties and unhook my bra. Neatly, I took all my clothes off, folded them with my bra and underwear tucked in between the folds , and placed them on the dresser.

I slipped under the covers and lay on my stomach.

"Trey, I am ready.

Trey entered the room. I could tell he was standing over me.

In his very sexy, deep voice, he said, "I am going to place my hands on your back and start the massage. At any time you feel too much pressure, let me know, and if you would like more pressure, I can give you more. Okay, Crystal?"

"Okay, Trey. I've been stressed, I am ready."

He slowly removed the covers from my shoulders and pulled them down to my waist. Next, he rubbed lotion between his hands.

"Take a deep breath for three seconds and let it out. Let all your stress out and relax."

He placed his hands on each side of my back and began to move them in long strokes from my shoulders to my waist, back and forth.

"Um, Crystal, your body is very tight. You are holding on to a lot of stress. You may feel some discomfort because your muscles are so tight. I want you to know it will get better with time and consistency."

As he massaged me, I began to think about my time in London at WCP industries and my breakup with Spencer. I felt a tear roll down my face, followed by another and another. A sniffle escaped from my nose with a sob.

"Crystal, is the pressure okay?" Trey whispered.

"Yes, the pressure is perfect, thank you."

As I lay on my stomach, enjoying the slow purposeful massage on my back, I began to open up to Trey about my relationship issues and my time at WCP Industries London office. He asked me no questions, just listened to me silently.

When I was done telling him my entire story, he said a few words to me that made me feel better.

"Do not love someone so deeply that it is not good for you, especially if he doesn't show you the same love you give him. It is time for you to take your life and live it to the fullest. You're too much of a woman to allow this man to keep you down. I need you to focus on loving yourself and stay focused on your goals."

I am well aware I don't need this man's or anyone else's validation, nonetheless, it was nice to hear.

"Thank you, Trey, I really appreciate your advice, and I'll take it to heart," I replied.

Trey gave me the best massage I ever had, and I felt so good once the sixty-minute massage was concluded.

I vowed to Trey that I would continue with my massages on a weekly basis, and whenever I was stressed. I left the studio feeling like a new woman, physically and mentally. I got in my car and immediately texted Chaundra.

Thank you for giving me the advice to get a massage. This is my first visit, and I feel great! By the way, my massage therapist is HOTTT!

That was how I met Trey, and that was the beginning of our massage therapist and client relationship. Our friendship developed, and I began to come to see him for massages weekly, sometimes twice a week. It didn't hurt to see him since he was gorgeous and gave me the best advice. I would never forget what he said to me at the end of my last massage session.

"Leaving a relationship is never easy. You may have lost a relationship with Spencer, but you gained something more valuable, your life! When you have a partner who does not deserve you, it is draining, and you realize they do not deserve to be in your life. Crystal, you have too much good in you for you to waste it on a man who does not recognize your contribution or appreciate your loving qualities."

Those words were exactly what I needed to hear before I started my new career in the Philadelphia office.

The next Day

I woke up to the lyrics of *Survivor* by Destiny's Child from my cell phone alarm. Today I was supposed to start my new position and leave my past behind. After getting out of bed, I walked to the bathroom to start showering.

Entering my spacious walk-in closet, I eyed the many blouses, pants, skirts, and blazers hanging neatly on the racks. I began to run my hands across the clothes, the fabrics brushing softly against my fingertips. Looking over the array of options, I still felt undecided about what to wear for my in-person interview. I thought about the TV shows featuring powerful women and the types of attire they wore.

After much consideration, I decided on a straight-lined skirt with a slit to the right, a crisp white blouse, and a matching blue blazer. I placed the trio against my body and looked into the full-length mirror. I smiled and said to myself out loud, "This is the outfit for my first day, nice and conservative. Perfect for the first impression at the Philly office."

Once I finished getting dressed, I looked back into the full-length mirror. I was so happy I had taken my mother's suggestion to wear an outfit like this for my final interview at WCP Industries.

I completed the look with an application of moisturizer, primer, and "warm chestnut" foundation. This outfit was perfect, not too sexy, and it looked like I was serious about business. I wanted to be hired for my work, not for the way I looked. Now that I had a chance to start a new career, I thought about what Trey would have wanted me to say. I whispered an affirmation to myself as I smiled at my reflection.

"Today I start loving myself more. I got this!"

"Crystal, are you up? You are going to be late for your first day," my mother yelled from the couch downstairs.

I walked downstairs to see my mother. I twirled around the landing of the steps so she could get a better view of me and give her approval on my interview attire.

"Mom, how do I look?" I called, walking into the living room.

My mother, Carol Harris, sat in front of the television on the plush brown sectional, watching her favorite reality show. This was the state my mom had been in since my father walked away from our family.

Her medium-length hair, peppered with grey strands she no longer bothered to dye, was pulled back with a hair tie at the nape of the neck. Her light brown eyes, which once had a sparkle, were now somber with exhaustion. They were accompanied by fine lines that traced along the corners of her mouth and eyes, which were only a few of the visible signs of her heartbreak. When she smiled, I could sometimes see the mom I once knew. The mom who had joy and hope in her eyes.

She wrapped her full figure in her favorite soft blanket and woolly socks. She was still attractive, but anyone could see that life had taken a toll on her beauty. She sipped on a mug with either tea, coffee, or wine. I wasn't quite sure what it was, but I didn't want to ask her because I didn't want to embarrass her. At one time, she was vivacious and confident. Now she constantly battled with self-doubt. I was happy to say she still had her witty sense of humor that surfaced sporadically, often to mask her phantom pain.

I thought the world of my mother; she always had my back. When I got a full-time position in London, she moved with me. She said it was way too far away for her to be away from her daughter. She packed up her belongings and put them in storage, then put the house up for rent. I loved that she was coming with me.

When I left the London office to move to WCP Industries in the US, she did not hesitate to move with me again. She was so supportive, she also understood the real reason I was leaving London. She knew it was due to a horrible breakup with Spencer William. There was no way I would continue to work in the same building as him.

"Crystal, sweetie, you look beautiful," she said, pulling her attention away from the two lovers on the television, fighting. "Darling, you look so pretty and professional, and it was a great idea for you to straighten your curls. It seems like the latest fashion is to wear your hair straight. That's what men like. You look stunning, baby, and everyone will think the same."

I frowned in the mirror, second-guessing my hairstyle.

"I have my second interview today. I want them to see my credentials, not my looks. Are you sure about this look?"

"Yes, Crystal, this is a very smart look, you'll do fine. Just relax and let them see the professional, qualified woman that's standing in front of me." Mom said confidently.

"Mom, why don't you take a walk? The weather is beautiful today. You look like you could use some sun."

Smiling, I walked over to her, gave her a kiss on her cheek, and proceeded out the door toward my car to go to my last interview at WCP Industries Philadelphia branch.

Leaving the house I smiled to myself, feeling very confident, I had this position. When I was in the London office. I was consistently praised for getting the high-end clients and closing the deal. Matter of fact, they called me the "Closer". I was not concerned about getting the position. I felt confident Mr. Jason Pfeiffer would review my credentials and be very happy to have me on his team.

As I drove to the office location, I kept saying one of my favorite affirmations, " *I am enough. I am smart. I attract positivity. I am confident. I attract opportunity. I am kind, I am worthy of good things. I got this job in the bag.* "

CHAPTER 2
Dean Palmer

I walked into the lobby of WCP Industries, Philadelphia branch, dressed to impress with a new grey tailored suit.

I look good, I thought, as I looked at my reflection in the glass door of the lobby.

I was smiling , feeling confident about the new management position that would be offered to me. I walked through the doors and saw my friend, Brian Smith, who was thirty-four years old and single. He was well known in the company for his savvy business strategies and even more well known for being the man with three baby mamas. Brian's handsome, chiseled jaw, almond complexion, and perfectly symmetric features seemed to attract the ladies. He was always dressed to impress.

I shook my head with a smirk before giving Brian a bro-hug.

"Hey, Brian, good to see you. Today is the day, brah. I am finally about to scoop that promotion. I have been grinding for years. I put in mad work, so I am walking in there knowing this promotion has got my name stamped on it."

"That's all you D. You've been putting numbers on the board non-stop, holding it down at every financial audit. You deserve this promotion.

That seat's already got your name imprinted." Brian folded his arms, smirking.

"Thanks, B, that means a lot coming from you. Once I get this position, I will be on a direct route to Executive Vice President. How I'm looking, though? Gotta make sure I kill it when I step into the VP's office," I said, as I smoothed out my red tie into place.

"Man, you're looking bossed up. Walk in there like you own the company. Let'em know you're ready for the promotion."

Brian clasped his hands together and began to smile.

"Dean, hold up. You peep that jawn that slid through, like fifteen minutes ago?"

"No, I did not see anyone. I guess I missed her. She must be new to the company" I admitted.

"Who are you talking about ? Don't tell me you mean shorty in the mailroom, cause I already tapped that last week."

Brian cracked up. "Ha Ha! You're wild. Nah, not her. And you foul for that. She is still on my list, though."

We both laughed and dapped each other in agreement.

"The Jawn I saw earlier was beautiful. She had long black hair pulled back in a ponytail. She had perfect features. She was the color of warm caramel, deep, dark black eyes, and sweet, luscious red lips that looked like they were on a permanent pucker. Her body was a ten, too. Legs for days, curves sitting right, and the body is tight! Beautiful perky tits. Brah, this lady was a ten plus!

I watched her switch her cute ass on the elevator. She could be my next baby mama." Brian said, chuckling.

"Ok, Brian, she sounds more like my type, but I am not thinking about women right now. I'm about to get this senior executive position. More importantly, you don't need another baby momma."

"I hear you," Brian said, nodding his head as he chuckled.

"Man, I gotta go. I'll holla at you later."

After parting ways with Brian, I walked over to the elevator. I was headed for the tenth floor, the executive level, and down the hall to the office of Vice President Jason Pfeiffer. I walked into the foyer of Mr. Pfeiffer's office where I saw a beautiful woman dressed in a long skirt. I wondered if that was the woman Brian was referring to. If she was the jawn he was speaking of then she is beautiful and sexy as hell.

She looked up at me with a smile and said hello as I took my seat in the leather chair next to her. I smiled and said, "Hello." Confused about who this woman could be, I concluded she must have be an admin assistant.

CRYSTAL

A strikingly handsome Korean man in his early thirties sat beside me. He stood about six feet two, with dark curly hair and beautiful eyes. When he greeted me, his dazzling smile revealed an adorable dimple, making it hard not to smile back. *I really hope I have the opportunity to work with him.*

Mr. Jason Pfeiffer's administrative assistant came out of the office and said, "Hello, Dean and Crystal. Mr. Pfeiffer is ready for both of you to come into the office.

I looked at Mr. Jason Pfeiffer's administrative assistant, confused. I couldn't understand why Mr. Pfeiffer would want to see both of us at the same time. Who is this guy next to me? Then I thought: *he must be my administrative assistant, and he wants him to meet me as his new boss. Well, at least he is not bad on the eyes.*

Walking into the grand office, I observed the two large windows that were ceiling-to-floor with large red drapes on either side. The windows gave a clear view of the Schuylkill River and the lights of boathouse row. To the left of the office, there was a full-size bar with an assortment of liquor. On the right side of the office was an artificial putting green. A wooden mantle held a picture of him on a boat with two very attractive older men who resembled him sailing a tall ship. In the center of the office was a large mahogany desk surrounded by expensive furniture.

I could get used to this.

Mr. Jason Pfeiffer smiled at us and told us to take one of the two leather seats in front of his desk. We both followed his command and sat down.

Mr. Jason Pfeiffer was surprisingly young-looking. I assumed he would be in his sixties, but the man who sat in front of me was in his early forties and handsome with olive skin, chiseled jaw, and sea blue eyes that sparkled. His short black hair was faded tight on the sides. He had a smile that lit up the room.

Dean and I returned the smile.

“Thank you, Mr. Pfeiffer, for taking the time to see me,” Dean said.

Mr. Pfeiffer smiled and said, "Please, call me JP. I am happy that both you and Crystal were able to come in at the same time. I am sure you are both wondering why I have both of you in my office. As you know, there is a position that needs to be filled. The position is a Senior Executive Director position in Marketing. The person who gets this position must be a leader who is comfortable delegating tasks and is a team player. Education is a priority and experience is a must. Most of all, I want the person who holds this position to take the Philadelphia branch to the next level. We need this branch to do better than the prior year. If we don’t see a change in sales, we may not have our jobs next year. Therefore, it is important for the next Executive Directors to make an impact on the sales bottom line. Now, with that being said, I need to ask both of you a question. If you had to, would you be able to work with each other without an issue?”

Dean thought about the question and responded, “Yes.”

I wasn't sure what Mr. Pfeiffer was getting at with the question, but I figured that he was going to introduce this gentleman as my new administrative assistant.

“Yes, Mr. Pfeiffer."

“That is good to hear. I want to offer you both positions. I will be awarding the position of Senior Executive Director of Marketing to you, Dean Palmer, and you, Crystal Harris. Congratulations!”

Dean and I sat there in silence with bewildered expressions on our faces.

“Excuse me, Mr. Pfeiffer, I am confused. For clarity, are you saying I have the position as Senior Executive Director of Marketing for WCP and Co., and this man next to me, Dean, will be my assistant?” I asked, confused.

With eyebrows furrowed and eyes narrowed in on me, Dean said irritably, “You're my administrative assistant, what are you talking about? I worked my ass off for this position. I will be *your* boss, Ms. Crystal Harris."

"No, you are not going to *my* boss. Who are you? You must be confused. Do you know what I accomplished when I was in London? My work speaks for itself," I retorted.

"Hold on, Dean and Crystal," Mr. Pfeiffer said, putting up both hands like a referee separating fighters. "I need to clear up some confusion. First, neither one of you will be an Administrative Assistant. I need someone with international experience to run as a Senior Executive Director, and that would be Crystal. Crystal has worked in our London office for the past three years, and she made quite the impression on the Senior Vice President, Spencer Williams. The London office has asked me to send her back. I know if they are asking for her, she is a jewel, and I am not giving her up."

"Mr. Pfeiffer, are you sure they have requested me back to London?"

This is very interesting, I thought.

After Spencer and I broke up, I never heard from him again.

Ignoring my question, Mr. Pfeiffer continued speaking. "More importantly, she made contacts with some of the largest clients, and her connections and great revenue generated from the deals she secured, well, let's say the company will be in an awesome position for the next ten decades. As I stated, education is a priority for this position."

I smiled with pride, hearing him speak of me. Taking a sneak peek at Dean, I could see him glaring at me with disdain.

Dean moved his attention to Mr. Pfeiffer and said, "Mr. Pfeiffer, with all due respect, I am really confused. Why am I here if you made a decision?"

Mr. Pfeiffer continued, "Well, Dean, I also believe that experience is a must. Dean, you are the most experienced. The expertise you bring to the table is invaluable and well-needed. I personally saw you work hard for this position, and your work ethic reminded me of myself ten years ago. I felt I couldn't have education without the experience. Therefore, you will both hold the title of Senior Executive Director for a while. You both agreed you could work as a team, so this will indicate whether you can be a team player for the benefit of the company. Will you be able to work together for a lengthy time?"

Dean and I looked at each other, and we both answered, "Yes," hesitantly.

"Great, and congratulations! I want you two to start working together immediately. I have two large offices for you, and you can get settled and start tomorrow morning as the 'Dream Team'. I will announce your positions tomorrow morning at the office so everyone will be on board. I will leave it up to you two to divide the responsibilities. In a few months, we will review your positions. I know this is not traditional, but you will come to learn I'm not a traditional person. Thank you for your time."

I couldn't believe Mr. Pfeiffer's decision. I wanted to argue the point that Dean was not needed. I would be enough for the company. At the same time, I didn't want to seem difficult.

Dean and I thanked Mr. Pfeiffer for the opportunity and shook his hand before we left his office.

I walked out to get to the elevator, unintentionally following Dean, who had just pushed the button. We were just standing there in silence, looking straight ahead at the silver doors of the elevator. Surely he was thinking about what we just agreed to.

Our shared silence was interrupted by the abrupt ding of the elevator arriving. When the doors opened, we both quickly stepped on. When the doors closed, I attempted to extend an olive branch.

"Hey, I know this isn't what we expected, but I would like for us to work together and get along. I'm willing to give this a try if you are." I offered.

Dean turned toward me and narrowed his eyes.

"Don't get comfortable, Crystal. You won't be here long. You might have Mr. Pfeiffer fooled with your cute school teacher look, but I'm not buying it. I will work with you because my job depends on it. Don't think for a second I'll be carrying you along and doing your work for you!"

My eyes widened with shock from his words before I matched his energy and narrowed my eyes back at him.

"Carry me? Dean, I thought I would have to carry you and teach you some fundamentals of being a director and making and closing deals. So don't get it twisted, pretty boy, because I have no problem straightening you out. You don't fool me. I know you're probably used to having things come easy for you with others making sure you are a success. I see about a hundred guys like you every day, fooling corporations and getting promoted due to their privilege. I'm not going anywhere, but to my new office. See you later, partner."

With that, I walked out the elevator with my head held high into the bright lobby while Dean was still picking up his jaw.

Dean

I was rendered speechless. Exiting WCP, I hailed a taxi home, to finish the day in my loft condo. While in the taxi, watching the city pass me by, I couldn't believe I had to share the responsibility of Sr. Executive with this new woman. I worked so hard for this job, and now a woman who didn't put in the time or the work was going to share in the responsibility. The taxi stopped in front of my condominium in Rittenhouse Square.

I gave the driver my usual 20% tip and went about my way to my condo. I felt so heavy making the trek to my front door. All the excitement and certainty I had this morning had completely disappeared. One thing I was for sure about was that I didn't trust that surprisingly sexy woman, and I would definitely be keeping an eye, or both, on her.

CHAPTER 3
Crystal

"Hey, Mom, I'm home."

Getting no response, I went into the living room. Just as I suspected, Mom was there, exactly where I left her, sleeping on the sofa while the TV played 90-Day Fiancé. I turned the television off and got a nearby blanket to cover her up before I gave her a gentle kiss.

"Good night, Mom."

Thinking about the day she must have had weighed on my heart. It had been fifteen years since my father left us, and still my mom showed signs of her anguish as though it happened yesterday. I remembered when my parents were happy. Staring at the picture on the mantle, I reflected back on the times when my father, Henry Harris, would pick me up, swing me around, and tell me he loved me.

Before he left, I had a very close relationship with my father. My father was everything to me. I was the definition of a Daddy's girl. Every day after elementary school, I would wait for him to come home from work so he could throw my little body in his arms and sing a song.

You are my Crystal, rare and strong,
A perfect gem where love belongs.
You are my Crystal, shining bright,
My heart's delight, my guiding light.

I absentmindedly hummed the little song whenever my thoughts landed on my father. On the day Mom was diagnosed with Cancer, my dad was devastated, but vowed that they would get over this hurdle together as a family.

Dad and I would take Mom to the hospital for treatment. After Mom started her chemotherapy, she would constantly vomit, and not always be able to make it to the bathroom. She got so thin and frail. I could see the stress on my father's face. The situation was taking its toll on all of us.

Eventually, I noticed that my dad was not coming home at the same time. He began to show up later and later. My dad made sure he took my mom to all her appointments, but became less available for all of her other needs. The responsibilities of taking care of Mom soon fell onto me. I would still look out of the window, waiting for my dad to come home. My heart would break every time he never showed.

Soon treatment was over, and Mom was getting better. She had fully recovered, and her doctor was so happy that the cancer was in remission. At twelve years old, I noticed that my father stopped coming home, and when he was there, he was less attentive to Mom. Ultimately, he no longer had time for me.

One day after school, I heard my parents yelling.

"Sorry, Carol, I can't help it, I gotta go. I love you, but it's not the same."

"Daddy, what is going on?"

"Hi, Crystal. I didn't know you were home. Baby, I love you, but Daddy has to leave for a while, and I will come back to see you. Mom and Daddy are not seeing eye to eye."

He bent down, hugged me, and kissed my head as he hummed my song. With tears in his eyes, he left the house. I ran after him, screaming for him to come back. He kept walking and never turned around.

I later found out that he began seeing one of the nurses who was taking care of Mom when she was in treatment. The nurse started off comforting my father every time he brought Mom to the hospital. She was fifteen years younger than him. I was fourteen years old when I found out my father had a new family. I was at the mall and saw him, his new wife, and his toddler looking like a happy family. My heart stopped when I saw my father pick up the toddler the same way he used to do to me and sing a little song.

It was on that day that I finally lost hope of my family being together again. I resented Henry Harris. I hated to see how his absence left my mother such a broken and lonely woman. She was always a good mother, but she never dated and never spent any time with friends. The only thing that seemed to make her happy was reality television. I vowed not to allow a man to have any control over my emotions. I refuse to let that happen to me.

My mind drifted to Dean. If Dean Palmer wanted a fight, he would get one. I won't give up this job; I have been through too much pain in life to allow him to take it from me.

Wait 'til he sees what this HOT school teacher can do.

CHAPTER 4
Dean

The next day, I arrived to work early. I wanted to make sure I got the better desk in the office that I now share with Crystal. Walking down the long hallway past Mr. Pfeiffer's office, I could see a light coming from *our* office. When I got inside, I caught Crystal decorating her desk and putting up file holders.

"What are you doing here so early, Crystal? Did the school let the teachers out early?" I teased, clearly agitated.

In a very sweet voice, Crystal replied, "Good morning, Dean. Nice to see you as well. Since you think I look like a schoolteacher, I guess I need to teach *you* that the early bird gets the worm. Consider me an eagle, my little sparrow," Crystal smirked.

I glared back at her. I couldn't tell if I was more frustrated or amused at the thought of me being her anything. I knew that Crystal was a person I wouldn't be able to underestimate. She evidently was a force to reckon with. Apparently, I hit a nerve telling her she looked like a schoolteacher. I chuckled to myself. She *was* a sexy schoolteacher, but I would never give her the satisfaction of telling her that.

I started to get down to business, unpacking my office supplies and organizing my desk. I couldn't help but wonder about my new "partner."

What a shame. Such a stunning woman with such a bad attitude. She won't get far here. I wonder what she did in the London office to make her so popular. If she was so great, why didn't she stay in London? There is more to Crystal Harris than she shows.

There was a knock at the door, and we turned around in shock.

"Hi, Dream Team. Mr. Pfeiffer would like to see you in his office," Judy, his assistant, announced.

I darted immediately toward the door to Mr. Pfeiffer's office, but not before Crystal had beaten me out. Here I was once again trailing behind the perfect ass of this frustrating woman. I couldn't help but watch as she quickly swished her hips in that skirt, trying so hard to walk as fast as she could professionally.

You win this time, Ms. Harris.

When I finally got to Mr. Pfeiffer's office door, Crystal knocked twice. A man's voice behind the door stated, "Come in." I still did the gentlemanly thing and opened the door for her. We entered to find Mr. Pfeiffer sitting at his desk, looking over some documents. I noticed he had a picture of himself skiing in the Alps, and in the picture were two gentlemen in the background smiling. The two men looked like they could be relatives.

The two men resembled the CEO of the WCP company strongly.

"You want to see me," Crystal asked in that same sweet voice.

"Good morning, Mr. Pfeiffer. Judy said you wanted to see *us*," I elaborated, emphasizing the us. Mr. Pfeiffer smiled.

"Yes, we have potential new clients for co-branding product coming to the office, and he wanted to meet the dream team that he'll be working with. Dean, you are great with numbers. He'll want to see what our company's data can do for business, so give him the data he needs to make him want to work with us. The point is for them to gain a new market in the States, etc.

"Mr. Pfeiffer, what country are they from, and can you give me more clarity?" Crystal asked inquisitively. Her interest had undeniably been piqued.

"Sure, Crystal, I will fill you in. I will be clearer. We have a product from our skin care line, and the other company's product can be combined with our product. I want our two products to work together to make one product, thus gaining customers from both companies, and gaining market nationally and internationally. I will give you more information later..."

I smirked. *I guess Crystal isn't as smart as she thought. I am sure Mr. Pfieffer is thinking she is asking a stupid question. Now he knows she has no clue about co-branding. Girl, you're pretty but not that useful, get ready to pack your bags.*

"About the nationality, Crystal, they are from England, and I thought your experience working in London would give us an advantage since you'll be able to connect with them on a more personal level. You know, talk about your experiences there, and make them feel at home while you build a relationship with them," Mr. Pfeiffer responded, looking at her like she was a missing piece to a puzzle.

Watching Crystal smile and nod her head in agreement, hanging on to every word, I realized I was going have to up my game. It was apparent that Mr. Pfeiffer actually saw her as a valuable employee.

I can't allow this woman to outwork me.

Crystal

"Ok, Dean and Crystal, I need you to address the following: Strategic Alignment, product development in co-branding, and integrated marketing campaigns. Highlight the benefits of cross-promotion leveraging. I have a report that will brief you on all the details of the joint venture. Working together as a team is a must! Think of yourself as two companies merging. Will this be a problem?" Mr. Pfeiffer paused and looked each of us in the eye, awaiting our answer.

I could see the eagerness in Dean's face. *He really looks handsome when he smiles. Smiling is something he needs to work on doing more often,* I thought. *He needs to leave corporate work to me. This pretty boy is not ready for me. Working with a client from the UK is right up my alley.*

Dean had a glimmer of excitement in his eyes, and we both looked at each other. We both were thinking *game* and looked back toward Mr. Pfeiffer.

"No, no, not at all. It will not be a problem, Mr. Pfeiffer," we said in unison.

That was weird, but at least he seemed to be on board.

"Look at you all, already thinking as one. That's exactly what I want to hear. That's why you're my dream team, and I know you'll be able to make the company shine. Okay, work out the plans with each other, and we will meet again next week to update me on your progress. This is a huge project and a great opportunity for you both. I know you both will not disappoint me, and please stop calling me Mr. Pfeiffer; people might think I'm like my creepy twin uncles, Hendrick and Kendrick. Call me JP."

Inside my head, I was shouting, *Yes, yes!* This was exactly the type of opportunity I had been waiting for in my career. I guess coming back home to the States was a good idea.

Mr. Pfeiffer, or JP, continued, "In addition to all that, you have the freedom to pick your team, so think on it and let me know who you pick. Each of you can choose two or three people to build your project team, and one shared legal associate. This will really show us your leadership skills, so don't let me down. Thanks, guys, go out there and make me proud."

Dean and I took a moment to thank JP for his time and the opportunity before heading to our office.

I glanced over at Dean. He looked so excited. He reminded me of a child getting his first candy bar. It was nice to see him in such a different light since he hardly ever smiled. One could even say he was hot when he smiles, showing off a beautiful set of white teeth and sexy ass dimple in his right cheek.

We walked together in our silent bliss. We both had a pep to our step. We both knew this was a good opportunity to show we deserved the promotion. Glancing up at his six-foot-plus frame, I saw the determination in his eyes. Entering our office, as I looked up at Dean, I took the opportunity to touch base with him.

"Well, Dean, this is a huge project. I hope we can put our differences aside and get to business." I offered.

"I agree, Crystal. First, let's go over the objectives Mr. Pfeiffer, I mean JP gave us, then I will choose the objectives I will lead."

Huh? He's gonna pick out what he wants?

That wasn't what I meant. I meant we were supposed to work

together as a team. After clearing my throat, I took a deep breath to stay calm.

Let's try this again.

"Dean, I think we should work as a team. You getting to choose your objectives while I'm left with the rest, is not team playing. I think we should go over the objectives together and choose what's best for each of us. It's important that we show JP a united front and that we can get along. Don't you agree?" I asked with a smile.

"I agree, Crystal. I see what you mean. Listen, we can work out the specifics a bit later. For now, let's work on picking out our team, and we can come together tomorrow with the names and work on objectives. This is a lot of work, we need to have a good team behind us for support, so I'm gonna work on interview questions for my prospects. I think you should do the same. We can talk strategy tomorrow. How does that sound?" Dean said enthusiastically, friendly almost.

"Ok, sounds good, Dean. Talk to you tomorrow I will be working from home the rest of the day."

I was feeling optimistic, even believing that Dean and I could work as a team. Dean seemed like he was on board with me. He was cordial and ready to start the assignment. I wondered if we didn't start as rivals, would we have a good working relationship. He seems like a very focused worker, and I admire his ability to step up. I needed some private time to review this assignment and do some research on the merging company. I will look into their CEO, President, and their marketing strategy without the distraction of the office.

Dean

I couldn't believe I got this opportunity. This was what I had been waiting for: a chance to show Mr. Pfeiffer, I mean JP, what I could do. I think Crystal might be ok.

My father would be so proud of me for getting this appointment. I would finally prove him wrong.

I couldn't stop thinking about the fact that he thought I was a loser. As a child, he never gave me any praise or acknowledgement. I could never live up to his standards of what a winner was. Now, I had a chance to be seen in a major way.

My mother was going to be so delighted for me. She was the opposite of my father; she nurtured me with the support I needed all my life. Her love and encouragement were almost enough to make up for my father's disdain. Her reassurance kept me going, for the most part. Whenever I had a project at elementary school, it was my mother who helped me with my projects. She and I would work late into the night to make sure it was done well. Her support continued through high school, when she always showed up to my games. She supported my love of music; she paid for private saxophone lessons, although my father thought it was a waste of time. In Korean, she would have me repeat, Da jal doel geoya, Naneum sarangbatgo itda , Nan nae gachileul al-a, which translates to: *Everything will be ok, I am loved, and I know my worth.* Those comforting affirmations got me through some tough times.

I finally got the opportunity to show them that I deserved to be one of the leaders in this company. I was so thrilled, I called Brian.

"Brian, man, come up to my office. I have great news."

"Ok, bro, I'll be right up."

Moments later, Brian entered my office. He greeted me with our usual handshake.

"Hey, bruh, what's going on?"

I told him I was leading a co-branding initiative with the Dermacore company, and I got to pick out my team.

Brian grinned wide.

"This is amazing. I am so happy for you. I remember when we both started together all those years back. We both had our sights on the CEO, looks like you are on your way! "

"Yeah, it was over five years ago. We were fresh from college and eager to get into the industry. I had my eyes on the prize, and I wasn't gonna give up. This was what I was talking about. This is gonna show the VP that I should be the next lead of this company. B, this is gonna be terrific. I'm even gonna work with legal. I've never worked with legal."

"Yo, Dean, that's great. Oh man, so who are you gonna have on your team?" he asked inquisitively

"If you're interested, you know for sure I would like you on my team."

Brian dapped me up. "For sure! You already know I'm interested. This is gonna be great. Wait a minute. What about that sexy Jawn, you know that sexy co-worker of yours?"

"Oh, you're talking about Crystal? She won't be a problem. I'm sure to outshine her. Speaking of which, stop referring to her as 'Sexy,' it's disturbing." I said that last part with a little more bite than I wanted.

"Yeah, yeah. I thought you and Crystal were going for the same position." Brian said, annoyingly curious.

"Yes, we are, but well, we're both working together on this project."

"I thought you said you were the lead?" he pointed out.

"I *am* the lead, but she's leading with me. So yes, we are co-leads on the project, but I'm not worried about her; she's no threat. I know I will dominate and be triumphant-- little miss school teacher is no match for me".

"No doubt, you'll be triumphant. This is a lot of responsibility, and if they thought you couldn't do it, they would not have offered you the opportunity. I'm hoping my shot will come soon, too."

"It will come soon, Brian, I know it," I assured him as he walked out of my office.

Walking out to the kitchenette, I saw Crystal on the phone, smiling. *Why is she so happy? Who is she talking to?* I worried.

Crystal looked over to me and said to the person on the other end of the phone, "Hey, Trey, I will be over to you soon. Bye."

"Hey Dean, I am about to leave. Do you need me?"

"Huh? Oh, umm, no. I'm good. Do you have any questions for me before you leave for the day?"

"Nope, nothing, thanks for asking." I heard her say as she swished in her skirt to the elevator.

I just stood there in the lobby watching her walk away.

Who was she talking to? Who's Trey? Is Trey her man? Why did her beautiful face light up while talking to Trey? Why do I feel jealous? She is my competition; I shouldn't feel so concerned about what Crystal does when not at work. I just couldn't stop picturing her pretty face smiling on the phone with Trey.

Why couldn't I get Crystal off my mind?

CHAPTER 5
Crystal

I was on cloud nine. Immediately after the meeting with Mr. Pfeiffer, I called my massage therapist, Trey, a.k.a. fake BF, and made an appointment with him. I literally just needed to share my good news with someone. I figured Trey was the best person. I really relied on Trey. He was a friend, a massage therapist. Honestly, I had no desire to have a relationship right now, but Trey was safe. He was always pleasant and so positive, not to mention he was gorgeous. Plus, he gave amazing massages.

As I walked up to the door of the studio, Trey greeted me.

"Hello, beautiful. Your smile has made my day. I am so glad you called for an appointment. What do you feel like today? Do you want a deep massage, a Swedish massage, or is this a day for cupping?" he asked with a handsome grin.

"Thanks, Trey, for taking me last minute. I just left work, and I felt like a massage was in order. I have no woes today, I just want to treat myself with a massage and your company," I said with a faint giggle

"No worries at all, it is always nice to have you. You know the routine, and let me know when you're ready for me to come into the room," he said as he walked out of the room.

Three minutes later, I was tucked under the covers naked and ready for my massage. I called Trey to come into the room to begin the massage. Trey entered the room with a tub of massage cream.

"So, Crystal, I have a new massage cream with lavender in it. Would you like to be the first to try it out?

"Yes, that sounds great, and can we do a Swedish massage today? I feel like it's a light day, and I want to tell you about my good news."

"Ok, I can't wait to hear all about it. Let's start this massage. The moisturizer might make you relaxed to the point where you will want to go to sleep," Trey warned.

"Ok, I'll hurry and tell you about my day, in case I fall asleep."

I began to tell Trey about my meeting with Mr. Pfeiffer and his proposal for Dean and me to lead the co-branding merger. As I went on about my day, I drifted off to sleep and slipped into a dream.

A deep seductive voice whispered in my ear from behind, as I made coffee in the kitchenette in the office of the WCP London office.

"Excuse me, Crystal. Do you mind if I bother you for a moment?" the deep voice questioned.

I nodded yes.

"I'd like to see you in my office when you have a moment." The mystery man's voice was deep, sexy, and the closeness of his breath on my ear caused chills to run up and down my spine.

I took a deep swallow. Keeping my back to him, I responded nervously, "Ye.. yess, sir, I will see you right away."

I thought, what could the sexy Mr. Spencer Williams want with me?

I worked at the WCP Industries London branch for a year, and Mr. Williams never noticed me. He never had too much to say to anyone in the office. He traveled to the United States often, so it was common not to see him. The word in the office is that he was single and every woman found him incredibly attractive.

I respected him for being so focused. Although I found him very attractive, I always maintained a professional demeanor. As I walked out of the bathroom toward his office, I figured he must have wanted to introduce me to next year's objectives. I walked to the door of his office, and my heart began to race. I leaned into the door and knocked twice.

I entered the office, and I saw Mr. Williams standing at his desk looking over documents.

"Mr. Williams, what can I do for you?" I asked confidently.

He looked up at me with his deep brown eyes, staring at me intently. His dark brown hair was cut short on the sides and lay perfectly on top of his head

"I want you to know that I am very impressed with you. I've been watching you, and your work has been impeccable. You've helped the company get into markets we have not been able to gain in the past. I would like to thank you personally."

Looking up at him in pleased astonishment, I smiled. I was surprised he recognized my achievements and hard work. Flattered, I said, "Thank you so much, Mr. Williams, for noticing."

Clearing his throat, he glided toward me and said, " Well, I would like to thank you more personally. Would you be open to having dinner with me so we can celebrate your achievements and talk about future endeavors?"

"Oh yes, Mr. Williams, yes, dinner would be delightful," I said brightly.

I will pick you up tomorrow around 7:00.

Yes, Mr. Williams, I mean Mr. Spencer, that will be fine," I said nervously.

"Great! See you tomorrow," Spencer said with a very handsome smirk.

The next day at 7:00p.m. "Good afternoon, Crystal. You look stunning," he said, grinning. He held his hand out to help me into the car. I placed my small, freshly manicured hand into his large hand as he guided me into the back seat of the car. I felt like a princess, and he was my prince, ready to take me away. I had never seen Spencer look so handsome, and that was saying something because this man was fine.

We entered the car, and his driver started the engine. Spencer leaned over to hover over my ear and said, " I hope you like the Core restaurant, I heard it is very good, and it earned a Michelin star," he said seductively

"This is a beautiful restaurant, thank you for inviting me," I said.

"It's my pleasure, I am happy you accepted my invitation. You also deserve a night out. Do you realize if it was not for you, we would have never gotten into the markets we are excelling in if it was not for your ingenuity," he said, matter-of-factly.

"Well, Mr. Williams, Spencer, I appreciate the opportunity, because if

you didn't believe in me, I would have never had the chance to make the relationships with the companies. I feel like I have a real knack for getting people to warm up to me and trust me."

During dinner, I spoke about my life in the US. When I tried to ask him about his childhood, he deflected back to me.

"It was a typical English childhood, nothing interesting," he shrugged. "I prefer to hear about you. You fascinate me, and I love your American accent!"

"Really? I always thought Brits sounded more charming--"

"You are beautiful," he interrupted. "I am absolutely taken by you, Crystal. I want to know you better. I think you are very interesting, and I have not had a woman catch my heart in years the way you have. I must admit I am quite attracted to every aspect of you. I only hope you feel the same way about me."

"Mr. Spencer, I am surprised, I must admit. I would like to get to know you better as well." I stammered.

"Good, you have made me very happy. I am going to take you home now, because If I spend any more time in your presence, I will not want to leave you," he confessed

Smiling at him, I said, "Yes, that sounds like a good idea. I feel the same way, Spencer."

We left the restaurant and Spencer, and I drove in the car holding hands in silence. When we got to my Flat, Spencer walked me to my door.

My eyes locked onto his dazzling brown eyes, and I nodded.

He caressed the back of my head and bent down to me, and his smooth lips pressed against my lips. I grabbed the back of his head to get better leverage on his mouth. We stood there for ten minutes kissing and touching each other's backs, and hugging.

He kissed my cheek and whispered in my ear, "Crystal darling, let's keep our relationship just between you and me. I don't want to be part of the gossip in the office."

I was so into him, too, and I could not believe I was dating Mr. Spencer Harris. Spencer Spencer..eeeek!"

"Crystal, Crystal, are you ok? You fell asleep during your massage, and you kept saying Spencer. I wasn't sure if I should wake you up," Trey said with concern.

"Yes, yes, um, I was dreaming about my past when I was in London, specifically about my first date with my ex-boyfriend. It seems like when I sleep, he floods my thoughts."

"Yes, darling, I remember. Are you ok? I know thinking of him might cause you some stress."

"I'm fine, the breakup was just so bizarre."

"Because you never had full closure, your subconscious is having you review the relationship," Trey said tenderly.

"I guess you're right, Trey. He was so into me, and I was into him. He was a true gentleman. I know he felt strongly for me because he never gave any other woman the time of day, and he really liked that I was real and not trying to impress him. We had great conversations, and he wanted to know about me."

"Crystal, you're doing a good job healing from this relationship. You have so many positive things happening to you. I want you to put all your energy into the new assignment you were just given. Your boss knows you're the right person for the job, and you know you are going to be a success. Get your thoughts together, don't let your past hold you back, and take away your focus. He is not worth it. Keep me updated on your progress. I want to support you so you can get a massage once a week if you need it. Don't hesitate to call me if you need me. I am here for you as your friend," Trey sincerely declared.

"Thank you, Trey, that is good advice. I am going to work on getting my staff together so I can start working on the merger. I am so grateful I came to see you today."

I left his massage studio feeling positive. I was going to try to put Spencer out of my mind and get my mind in the game to focus on Dean, I mean, my new assignment.

CHAPTER 6
Crystal

A week later, at work, I had a one-on-one with Mr. Pfeiffer to give him an update on my plans with the client.

"Hello, JP. I have a meeting with the client today, as a matter of fact, within the next hour. I invited them to come to the office so I could show them that we're not your run-of-the-mill company. I know they're not a conventional type of company either. I researched that they liked for their employees to dress down, and they allow their dogs to come to work. In fact, I found out that the President, Liam Russell, has a fondness for Old English sheepdogs. When he was a child, someone in his family had one, and he loved it dearly."

Mr. Pfeiffer chuckled. "Crystal, you are amazing," he said. "You think outside the box. I knew you would be perfect to make that special connection."

I blushed and smiled at my boss, brimming with pride. "That's not all," I continued, "I invited their President and their team for a real English Tea! We're going to have tea sandwiches, biscuits, and herbal tea. My administrative assistant, Sophia Knowles, will help. She and I have called a caterer to bring in the food and she will be brewing the tea. Sophia brought in her own sheep dog, Sugar, for an added touch

"You are giving him a little England in Philly with those little sandwiches and tea.. Ha ha ha. That's perfect! Ha ha ha ha, and an old English Sheep dog. Simply brilliant! I can't wait for you two to meet. I know you will charm their socks off," Mr. Pfeiffer boasted, walking back to his office.

I went into the conference room to make sure it was all set up for our guests.

I wondered if I should have shared with Dean that I was bringing in the client. Over the past few weeks, he has been disrespectful at team meetings. He has been talking over me and repeating my statements, as if they were not understood when I said them the first time. Should I inform him of my meeting with Liam?

Nope! Ha ha ha! I know he wouldn't have informed me of his moves. Just in case, I left a message on his voicemail at his office line.

I checked my Bluetooth and made sure to connect my iPhone to my speaker, and decided to play 1990s hits like Pearl Jam, Tracy Chapman, Arrested Development, and Red Hot Chili Peppers. I figured Mr. Russell was in his mid-40s, and he grew up on this type of music. I hit play, and the melody poured out of the speakers. I had to admit this music was the bomb; I could really get into it.

Looking at my watch, I noticed I had a few minutes before they arrived. I decided to walk to the ladies' room for one more check of my appearance.

The door swung open to the bathroom, and strolling right in was my assistant, Sophia.

"Hey Sophia, how are you making out with getting the tea together?"

"I'm great. I decided to offer three varieties of tea: Earl Grey, English Breakfast, and Mint tea."

I got lucky getting Sophia to be a part of this project with me. Not only was she a good assistant, but she was well organized and always ready to take on a challenge. I would really like to see her move up with the company.

"Thank you, Sophia, that sounds perfect."

Sophia smiled and walked over to the full-length mirror. Sophia was the total opposite of me. She had short reddish-brown hair with a blonde streak in the front. She changed the color of her hair often. She wore colorful clothing and was very fashionable. Today she wore a yellow dress with a large red, blue, and green flower print. The color looked beautiful on her. It made her warm, chocolate-colored complexion glow. She paired the dress with large chunky red wedges. She had no problem putting makeup on her pretty face. She wore light yellow eye shadow, black eyeliner, and her face had contouring at the cheekbone, with red lipstick. She was beautiful with dark caramel skin and the longest, thickest eyelashes I have ever seen. She looked like she should be a fashion model. She loved running marathons and eating a hundred percent vegan, which showed in her slender figure.

"They should be here soon, Sophia. Will you be able to meet them in the lobby and bring them to me in the conference room?"

"No problem. FYI, I took Sugar outside to do her business, and she will be sitting in the conference room with you.

"Thank you," I said, impressed. "Sophia, I would really like for you to sit in on our meeting, so make sure you come in and join us. I really appreciate all your efforts."

Sophia smiled and hugged me, and before softly saying, "I got you, girl, more than you know. I want you to win in this company." I returned her warm embrace.

My phone buzzed, and I saw I had a text from Sophia notifying me that she was on her way with the client.

"Good day, Mr. Russell, it is kind of you to come to see us."

"Hello, Crystal. Thank you for having us."

"We are really excited about being here," I said with a warm smile.

"Allow me to introduce you to my executive of marketing, Stan Boyle. Feel free to call me Charlie."

"Good day, Stan. It's so nice to meet you."

Stan looked over his glasses at me and said, "Oh, it's nice to meet you, Ms. Harris," he said with a smile.

"I noticed you said that you were from England. Can you tell me exactly where, because I don't hear a British accent?" asked Mr. Russell.

"Yes, well, I grew up here in the States, but I worked in London for a few years, the first year was an internship, and after the internship, I was rewarded a full-time permanent position with the company. I lived in Greenwich."

Mr. Russell looked over at the table of food. "Oh, I see, and what is this I see over there?" He pointed to the tea sandwiches.

"Yes, on the table I have some sandwiches, pastries, scones, and some sweets. My assistant will be serving us tea as well."

"Impressive," Charlie laughed. "This is a real English tea. You make me feel like I am at home."

"I'm delighted you feel that way." I smiled, trying to contain my pride.

"Is that an Old English sheepdog in the corner? Oh my Lord, I can't believe it. I used to have one when I was a little lad, you know my granny, oh my grandma, bless her soul, I would play with it all day. I love to spend time with Granny," Mr. Liam said delightedly. "I would play with her all day. I tell you that dog was my best friend. Her name was Lizzy. Oh, I loved Lizzy so much. You know, sheepdogs are one of the best dogs to have in a family, and when it comes to herding and loyalty, no dog is better. What is his name?"

Rubbing behind her ear as she sat next to me on the floor, I told him, "Her name is Sugar for her sweet personality. She's from a champion line. Her owner is my assistant, Sophia Knowles, your escort to the conference room."

Sophia walked over from the entrance of the conference room. She was a stunningly beautiful woman, and I saw Liam's face light up upon seeing her.

"Nice to meet you, officially," Sophia said, holding her hand out for a handshake.

Grinning like a kid had their eyes on their favorite candy, Mr. Russell said, "Nice to meet you, Sophia. I cannot believe that you have an Old English sheepdog. That was my favorite dog growing up. Do you mind if I pet Sugar?"

"No, not at all," Sophia gently answered.

Sophia grabbed Sugar's pink leash and guided her over to Mr. Russell. He stooped to the floor, got on his knees, and started rubbing Sugar's head while he spoke to her in a shockingly adorable baby voice.

All the while, Sugar just looked at him, with her tongue hanging from the right side of her mouth.

"You just look so pretty, look at you, your black and white fur is groomed so well! You're a good girl, yes, you are," he cooed. Sugar responded with pleasure by wagging her nub of a tail back and forth. To everyone's surprise, Sugar began to lick Mr. Russell's face, and he loved it.

Stan Boyles was enjoying the assortment of food, his attention focused on nibbling a scone.

I was so pleased with how this meeting was going already. No need to talk about figures and business, we needed to connect and build relationships. My specialty. When I was in the London office, building relationships was the key to my success!

Everything was going perfectly. Mr. Russell was on the floor, hugging and loving up on Sugar. He kept looking at Sophia and then Sugar. It looked like he wasn't sure who he should give his attention to. The marketing exec was having a wonderful time over at the buffet. I sat there on the sofa, watching the scene and knowing I had made a smart choice by having this tea party and bringing Sugar and Sophia to the meeting.

Suddenly, the door opened to the conference room. Dean appeared at the door. He was dressed in a blue suit that fit him perfectly. He looked quite handsome standing in the doorway. He stood there for a moment, taking in the scene. His eyes locked on me, giving a cold glare.

"Excuse me, what is going on here?"

"Hello, Dean, this is Dermacore's President, Liam Russell, from the company we are working with to create a joint..."

Dean abruptly cut me off. "I know exactly who he is, Crystal."

I immediately sensed Dean's irritation.

"Ok, this is his marketing director, Stan Boyle," I interject matter-of-factly.

Still irritated, Dean questioned, "I'm confused. Why are you here? I mean, did I miss a meeting on my calendar? We are supposed to work together, partner."

Together? We are independently on a joint venture. Why is Dean trying to make me sound shady?

I looked over at Liam, and he wasn't paying any attention to Dean's words. He was more concerned with teaching Sugar to high-five him.

"Dean, I'm happy you made it to lunch. I wanted to meet with Liam before starting the business. Just a little meet and greet so he can get to know who he will be working with, you know, having a nice time chit-chatting over English tea and refreshments. This is Sophia's dog, Sugar, as you know, she likes to come into the office," I said matter-of-factly.

I hoped Dean would play along and not sell me out by revealing that we don't have dogs in the office.

To my surprise, Dean smiled, following my lead. "Yes, I remember, Sugar, good ole boy."

"Yes, she is a good Ole Girl," I emphasized.

"Do you mind if I join you, Crystal?" he said condescendingly.

"No, I don't have a problem with that. Come and take a seat," I invited him by extending my hand toward a seat.

Sophia walked over to him. "Well, I'm about to get tea. Would you like some?" Sophia asked Dean.

"Sure, I'll have some tea. It is a tea party, isn't it?" Dean said, annoyed.

"Ok, so I have some specialty teas, Smooth Move, Earl Grey, and English breakfast? "

"Get me a smooth tea, Sophia, thank you."

"Will do." Sophia walked out of the room with a smirk.

Navigating around Mr. Russell playing with Sugar, Dean walked over to the sofa and sat next to me.

He discreetly moved close to my ear and whispered, "You are so sneaky, Crystal Harris. You had Mr. Russell here at the office and didn't bother to tell me. I'm surprised at you! I thought you had more class than that, Crystal."

With him so close to my ear, I could feel his breath against the side of my face. I felt a warm feeling in my cheeks.

Smiling and speaking under my breath, ensuring Stan didn't hear me between bites of tea sandwiches, I bit back, "Dean, stop acting like we're a team. We both have our individual assignments, and I excel in creating relationships in the corporate world. I am working on my craft and my assignment. Honestly, you had nothing to do with this meeting. You had a chance to do the same. Stop hating, it's not a good look on you, by the way, check your office voice mail, I left you a message."

Dean leaned closer, and I almost got distracted by the intoxicating aroma of his cologne. Damn, he smelled delicious. The warmth of his breath tickled my ears.

Dean whispered, "I'm not hating. You're right, I could have done the same. It just seems odd that I had to hear from Brian that you were entertaining the same people we are supposed to work with. You just look so desperate and afraid I will show you up. Crystal, your pretty school teacher act will only get you so far. I suggest you give up now."

Huh, Dean thinks I am pretty, I thought. *Give Up?* I couldn't believe he said that. Ughhh, the ego on Dean was incredible. I had to fight to remember that he wanted me to give up. I hated that knowing he thought I was pretty gave me a bit of a thrill. I needed to keep the rivalry front and center. Before I could give him a piece of my mind, Sophia pleasantly entered the room.

"Hello, everyone, I am back with tea."

Dean and I glared at each other before returning our attention to Mr. Russell

Mr. Russell excused himself to wash up, and Stan took his seat at the table. Sophia placed the three Earl Greys on the table and one Smooth Move for Dean.

When Mr. Russell took his seat, we began to sip our tea. The room was silent. I seized the opportunity to break the silence.

"Mr. Russell, Stan, since you're visiting the States, do you have plans to visit any tourist attractions?"

"Yes, we're going to be visiting the Liberty Bell and Independence Hall. Philadelphia is the birthplace of the nation, right? Haha, we're jolly well looking forward to it."

"I would love to show you some of the other hidden jewels the area has to offer."

"Oh, Crystal, you are such a delight. I would love for you to show us around. Do you think Sophia would accompany us as well?" Mr. Russell beamed.

Sophia looked up with a smile and a slight nod of her head.

After making plans, the conversation between us flowed. Dean didn't contribute much, which was fine. Stan continued sampling all the food. I was stunned when Dean decided to join in on our enjoyable little chat.

"Mr. Russell, I would like to share with you our quarterly profits and some of the financial data I accumulated. The data will show how we can work together to increase sales."

"What's your name again?"

I fought to keep my laugh to myself. What was he thinking, blurting all that out like that?

"Dean Palmer, sir," he uttered

"Well, Dean, I don't want to disturb the vibe by bringing in data, statistics, and all those numbers. We appreciate Crystal setting up this English tea for us. I feel like I'm at home. We have had a fabulous time meeting you both. I would be willing to come back tomorrow and hear all about the numbers on two conditions: One, we have another lovely meal like this one. Two, Sugar and Sophia are present, along with Ms. Crystal.

"Yes, absolutely, we can have all conditions met. Thank you for the opportunity, sir," Dean said eagerly.

Dean and I escorted Mr. Russell and Stan to the descending elevator to the lobby.

"Enjoy the rest of your day. I look forward to seeing you tomorrow," I said cheerfully.

Dean walked away from me with no words. I guess he was pissed at me. I didn't want to upset him, but I do better when I am alone. I didn't need him messing it up for me. And no disrespect to him, but I crushed it today. He should have been grateful I set us up so well.

"Hey, Sophia, can you come upstairs with me? I want to ask you a few questions about Dean." I requested.

"It is about time. Let's get some of the leftover desserts, coffee, and tea," she giggled.

I felt comfortable confiding in Sophia. When Sophia and I met, she was so happy to work for a sister. We really hit it off, and we both believe in supporting women in business. I knew I could trust Sophia. We had gotten close during my time here, and while organizing the tea. Once we got settled in my office, I began my inquisition.

"I usually don't like to ask about people's personal business or their backstory 'cause I kinda take people for how they treat me, but I'm so confused about Dean Palmer. Can you give me some insight into his background? I just don't. I just don't get him. I want us to work well together, so whatever information you can give me will maybe help me understand him better. I feel like he is skeptical of me and thinks the worst. He whispered in my ear that I was sneaky because I didn't inform him of my meeting, but I knew if he was there, he would try to compete, and I could not make the necessary connection. I felt it would work best as a solo mission." I confessed.

"I've known Dean for several years. Right after college, Dean came to WCP. He started in an entry-level position with a few other associates, Brian Smith and Zara Ali. The team was determined to move up the corporate ladder, but Dean soared above them both. He first became a specialist, then a junior executive. Dean became romantically involved with Zara soon after they started working together. Brian had no one special in his life; he just dated around a lot. Dean and Zara soon became 'that couple' at the office." Sophia used her two fingers to make the quotation marks. My eyes were growing wide with all this info. She continued, "They were always together, inside and outside work. It was rumored that they even moved in together. I think that was just a rumor, it was never proven. The two were very much in love. Zara soon moved up to the junior executive level, followed by Brian. They were like the three musketeers. All three of us were good friends and stayed close.

Dean was planning to propose, but that week, Dean had an emergency. He had to go back to his parents' home, so he left for two weeks during that time. Brian was very busy covering Dean's assignments and chasing tail. Zara was left working and having a lot of time on her hands in Dean's absence. It was rumored that Zara was seen at a bar on Sansom Street. downtown with an older man. When Dean returned from visiting his parents, he seemed so happy to be back at WCP.

One night, he went to Zara's apartment to surprise her. When he got there, she wasn't there and looked like she hadn't been there for a few days, seeing the amount of mail that was piled up. He went to Brian to ask him if he had seen Zara. Brian informed him he'd been so busy covering both assignments and had only seen her at work. He thought she might have had an assignment on a new project because she had been going to the executive-level offices a few times.

Dean thought that was odd, but he would ask her about going to the executive level. Dean was able to finally communicate with Zara the next day. They both agreed to meet at their favorite restaurant to catch up on the past few weeks. Dean told her that his father had been sick, his mother needed his help, and he wanted to make sure he was there to support his mother. Zara filled him in on the work duties that happened while he was away. Dean questioned her about a special assignment Brian mentioned."

Sophia paused the story and rolled her eyes with a slight twist of the mouth. "I know all this information because Brian told me how it went down."

"Zara said the President of Marketing had been mentoring her and showing her what goes on at the senior executive level. Dean said he was proud of her. They had dinner and talked about some of the things they were going to do in the coming week before dessert came. Dean pulled a small box out of his jacket and placed it on the table. He proposed to Zara. In response, she said something really stupid. *'Oh, Dean, I don't know, I mean, I love you, but I'm not ready for marriage. Matter fact, I was thinking, maybe we should take a break for a while.'*

Sophia shook her head and continued the story.

"Dean was devastated, according to Brian. He was confused because he thought they were on the same page with the relationship."

I interrupted the story, "Sophia, this is so sad. She broke his heart? No wonder he's not very trusting."

"Yeah, girl, it was so sad. Everyone at the office felt bad for Dean. He was such a nice guy and so eager to please Zara. Everyone at the office disliked her after that. Dean returned to work the next day, but it was clear that he was very disturbed working around her. He didn't understand why she wanted to end the relationship so abruptly. He finally put it all together. While he was taking care of his parents, she had cheated on him and started a relationship with the marketing president. The sad part was that he grew distant and stopped dating for a long time. He would go on a date occasionally, but he never trusted a woman enough to become serious after Zara."

Maybe I should give Dean a second chance, I thought, *after hearing his story. Dean may not be as bad as I think. The man with the handsome smile might be more than he shows.*

CHAPTER 7
Dean

THE NEXT DAY- PRESENTATION

I walked into the conference room wearing my success outfit: a new blue suit, a white shirt, and my grey dress shoes. Mr. Russell and his associates from Dermacore Cosmetics would be eager to hear all I've got for them. I had been prepping for this meeting for a while, and seeing Crystal's sneaky maneuver yesterday made me even more determined to win over Dermacore Cosmetics.

I adjusted my red patterned tie and stepped into the packed room. Waiting inside was Crystal, Sophia, JP, Stan, and Mr. Russell, along with three of his associates. Oh, and that dog, Sugar. I narrowed my eyes on the dog. The dog was a distraction. Looking over at Mr. Russell, he had the dog at his feet, petting the top of its head. Crystal was sitting right next to Mr. Russell with a sweet smile on her face, looking pleased and innocent. I knew this woman was anything but innocent. She was no different than any of the other women I have known vipers with a pretty smile, excluding my dear mother, of course.

I headed over to Mr. Liam to greet him. Although I was confident with my presentation, I could feel my stomach turn upside down. Last night, my stomach was making a lot of noise. I ignored it, taking it as bad nerves from being so upset with Crystal. *I hope I'm not getting sick.* The eight people in the room barely glanced up.

Noticing I needed to get their attention, I began to clear my throat so my presence could be acknowledged. Crystal looked at me with a big, pretty smile. Damn, that woman was attractive.

"Dean, you're here, wonderful. Mr. Russell and I were just talking about some of our favorite areas to eat in London while we were waiting for you. We're ready when you are."

Ok, Ok. I got it. You guys are besties now. I see she has seduced Mr. Russell with her beautiful smile and charming, witty conversation. I hope he isn't weak and is about to fall for her charm, instead of my logic and good business sense. You won't have your fangs in him long, you sexyl viper.

"Hello, everyone," I said, acknowledging them all with eye contact and a smile. "What do you mean, waiting for me? I'm early. We weren't supposed to start until noon, but it's currently 11:30." Although my stomach flipped again, I didn't drop the smile.

What did you pull this time, Crystal?

"Oh, didn't you get my text? I sent you a message last night. I changed the time to 10:30 am so we can have time to eat and talk casually before the presentation. Since I had the pleasure of meeting Mr. Russell yesterday, I wanted to extend the same courtesy to you. A time for you two to get to know each other better." Crystal said, her smile ever-present.

"Oh, Crystal, you are a gem. You are as sweet as you are kind and thoughtful. If I had a daughter, I would hope she would have your attributes. You and Sugar here have made my time in the States so welcoming. Let's get on with Mr. Palmer's presentation." Mr. Russell interjected.

Well, played, Crystal. Now you've made me look incompetent for showing up late.

"Crystal, I didn't get that message. Thank you for thinking of me. I would love to get started." I said with a stiff smile.

"Yes, Dean. Let's get started." Mr. Pfeiffer said, "We're all very interested in your presentation. Shall we?"

PowerPoint slides flashed behind me, but I didn't need them—not for this.

"Ladies and gentlemen," I began, "imagine a single daily cream that hydrates your skin and feels like silk, soothes your skin like cool cucumbers, as well as leaves your skin radiant and looking younger. There is one thing that most lotions lack, and it is primal attraction. What do I mean by primal attraction? The WCP industries have a patent serum that uses each person's pheromones to find the right person to attract to you.

Currently, the role of pheromones in human attraction is often a debated topic. There is strong evidence on how pheromones work in the animal kingdom, but many scientists question how they work with humans.

WCP has used the best science and nature to come up with a serum that not only attracts the sexes but also attracts the right person to you —a serum where you can match two people that match physically, mentally, spiritually, and emotionally. Think about the perfect mate for you. This eliminates dating swipes, blind dates, coaching, etc.

Who are your ideal customers? Matchmakers. They get paid to find people's perfect match. Think of all the sites, resorts, and services that we can market to. When we combine the high-end Dermacore beauty cream with our serum, you have created a well-known and luxurious product. Imagine being the first and only company to have this exclusive product!"

There was a shuffle of suits. A senior atwho was skeptical about the merger with, Dermacore narrowed his eyes. "You're suggesting we merge with Dermacore and WCP industries? We'd be swimming in legal—"

"I'm suggesting we outsmart the market," I interrupted smoothly. "Dermacore brings the luxury. WCP has the medical legalities sorted, as well as the influencer crowd. Alone, we're brands. Together, we're a movement. It's not a product, it's a revolution."

Silence. Stan said, "And you've got data to back this revolution?"

I clicked to the final slide: a colorful mockup of the Pheraglow bottle beside a graph climbing like a rocket. "Consumer testing says they'll line up for it. All generations find that this is the answer. Millennials said, 'Finally, not a boring app.' Boomers called it 'the cure to loneliness.' Gen Z? They call it the 'solution.'"

Everyone in the room leaned in. I knew I had them.

Suddenly, I had a horrible cramp. I immediately grabbed my stomach in gut-wrenching pain.

"Are you ok, son?" I heard Mr. Russell ask with concern.

"I don't know, just a sharp pain in my stomach. I think it'll go away. Maybe it's jitters."

"No need to be nervous, son, that was a great presentation, I love the idea," Mr. Russell said.

"Yes, excellent job, Dean," exclaimed JP.

"You probably just need to go to the bathroom," Sophia whispered.

She must have seen something on my face that made her immediately jump up and grab my shoulders to guide me out of the conference room.

"Come with me, Dean. I'll help you to the bathroom," Sophia whispered.

Doubled over in one of the worst pains I ever had, I began to walk to the exit. Before I reached the door, I saw Brian enter the conference room.

"Hi, everyone, I have a friend for Sugar. Meet Max. I think you will love him, Mr. Russell. He's an American Staffordshire." Brian offered.

Looking at Brian in pain as I walked to the door," What are you doing, Brian?"

"Brian, put that dog away. We don't need your dog," Crystal said

"Don't you see I am here trying to help Dean to the restroom, he is not feeling good," Sophia snapped at Brian.

"No, Sophia, Dean is my friend, I will take him to the bathroom," Brian growled.

Brian and Sophia began to manhandle me to take me to the bathroom. While they argued over me and kept pulling me back and forth, Max, the American Staffordshire, got loose.

Max was running toward Mr. Liam.

Mr. Liam bent over and said, "Hey there, big guy, come here. Max, come here."

Max ran toward Mr. Liam, and Sugar growled in a protective nature. Max stopped running and eyed up Sugar. Sugar eyed him up.

Before you knew it, there was a full chase of dogs running all over the conference room, and a cacophony of both dogs barking and people yelling at them. Crystal was running after both dogs, and Mr. Liam was calling after Sugar. JP looked shocked and was trying to calm down the rest of the Dermacore executives.

Crystal screamed, "Get the table of food!" I looked at the 6 ft table that held scones, biscuits, and tea sandwiches, with iced tea. Somehow Sugar got the tablecloth hooked to her, and as she ran away from the table, all the food was scattered all over the floor.

I was stunned by the mess, but my own desperate situation was finally coming to an end. As I started taking steps out of the room, eager to get to the restroom without Sophia and Brian, a pressure like no other came through my backside and a warm feeling entered my pants.

I roared at Brian and Sophia, "Leave me alone, get the dogs!"

Brian, tearing his eyes away from the chaos in the room, took notice of me. "Sorry, Dean, I'll help you. Wait, what is that horrible smell? Did you shit yourself, bro? "

Desperate to get out of the room before anyone noticed my condition, I said between my teeth, "Yes, I did, and I would appreciate it if you stop talking so loud", as I looked towards Sophia.

"Hey, Brian, I think you should help Dean, and I am going to assist Crystal with this mess," Sophia said, walking off towards the chaos.

As soon as Brian and I walked out of the doorway, we heard a yell behind us.

"Nooooo, Max, No! She is a lady!" Mr. Liam yelled.

Everyone stopped and looked in the direction Mr. Liam was yelling. All you could hear was gasping. In the corner was Sugar standing still, with Max on his hind legs and his front legs locked into Sugar's back. He humped her from behind with vigor.

It was an awful sight, as everyone stood with expressions of shock or horror on their face as they watched Max go to town, with every thrust.

"Ughhh, they're mating", I heard someone scream

This was a disaster. I left the room and made it to the bathroom to be by myself.

How did this presentation go so wrong? Up until a minute ago, I knew the Dermacore group was loving my presentation.

Crystal

I returned to the scene of the crime after yesterday's disastrous presentation. In the corner of the conference room, I could hear a noise in the rear corner. I saw the service woman scrubbing the cake out of the carpet. I felt so bad for her. The room was still in shambles. This was all Dean's fault. I looked at the screen where Dean had projected his PowerPoint and the chair where Mr. Russell had sat, listening to Dean give his presentation on why we should merge products. He did an excellent job until he got sick. I don't know what was going on with his stomach, but apparently it must've been very painful because he was doubled over with a tortured look on his normally handsome face.

I couldn't understand why Dean thought it was a good idea to have Brian bring in another dog. Sugar was just sitting there, being a lady, and minding her business, and Max came up to her and started acting up. Food was flying in the air. Mr. Russell was screaming. JP was trying to calm everyone down, and Dean was trying to get to the bathroom. It was a complete failure. I felt awful, knowing that Dean and I were going to be fired. It was a disaster.

The next morning, I dreaded entering the office. Looking down at my watch, I saw it was getting close to nine. I started the walk to the elevator to go to the 6th floor. Dean was there waiting.

"Good morning, Dean."

Dean curtly replied, "Crystal," not making eye contact with me.

Sensing the tension in his voice, I tried offering an olive branch.

"How are you feeling today? Is your stomach better?"

Dean turned his body toward me and narrowed his eyes. "I'm feeling better. I don't know what you fed me the other day, but it made me sick. Or was that your plan to make me look weak in front of Mr. Liam Russell?"

The silver elevator doors opened, and we both stepped inside.

The doors closed, and I immediately looked him in the eye, defensively.

"I did nothing to you, I don't know why you were sick, not my problem, not my issue! I want to know why you ruined the meeting with that dog? If it weren't for that dog, Max, it wouldn't have been a disaster. I know you and Brian thought of that scheme together."

"Nope, wrong! I never told Brian to bring his dog. Brian made up his mind to bring Max." Dean snapped

The sound of the bell from the elevator, indicating we arrived at our selected floor, got our attention. The elevators opened. We both walked off in silence as we approached the doors of JP's office. Behind us, we heard his assistant say, "Mr. Pfeiffer is waiting for you. Go ahead."

Entering the room, I could feel the tension in the air. JP sat behind his desk, scowling as he watched Dean and me enter the room. I could tell he was very upset with us, as he did not offer us a seat as he had done in the past.

"Thank you for coming to my office. I wanted to talk to you about the meeting yesterday. I think we can all come to the conclusion that it was a disaster and an absolute disgrace.

I have never been in a situation where two employees of mine conducted themselves in such a horrible way."

"JP, sir, with all due respect, what part do you think I had with that disaster?" I questioned defensively.

Dean glared at me and shook his head in disgust.

Crystal, from my understanding, you tried to sabotage Dean's presentation by giving him something to upset his stomach at the tea you hosted, from what I was told.

"But I didn't give him tea--"

"Please, Crystal, don't interrupt me. From my understanding You two have been up to shenanigans ever since I gave you the assignment. Dean, I heard you had a secret meeting with the staff, handed out assignments, and left out Crystal and her assistant, Sophia. I witnessed you both cutting off each other at meetings and trying to dominate the conversation. You both have left each other off important emails. I have been watching both of you closely. I did not step in because I was hoping you two would act as a team and not enemies, and one of you would be the bigger person. Crystal, you should never have left Dean out of the meeting with Liam Russell. In regard to the second dog at the meeting, I am looking at your team, Dean. What a disaster, so disappointing. You are both equally to blame.JP leaned back in his chair and appraised us. His expression showed nothing but irritation and possibly a touch of craftiness.' JP blurted.

Dean and I both lowered our heads a little in shame at hearing JP's words.

"I had to do a lot of cleaning up with Mr. Russell. He was not happy to say the least. I was able to hold on to the partnership without any help from you two. The question is, what do I do with you two now?"

"I had to reach out to my uncles, Hendrick and Kendrick Pfeiffer, to see what they thought I should do. I'm gonna be honest with you. I was going to terminate both of you. After speaking to them, I had a change of heart. My uncle, Kendrick, and Hendrick Pfieffer, CEO of WCP Industries, suggested a different course. They led me to understand the value that you both still have to offer to the company. Against my better judgment. I'm going to take their advice."

Simultaneously, Dean and I exhaled and looked at JP eagerly, thankful that termination was off the table. *His uncle Hendrik, is the CEO of the company; I would of never thought we would get this attention.*

"I'm going to force my two superstars to work together, so here's the plan. You both will be going on a camping trip together. You will be forced to work together for survival, and if you don't work together, you may not survive, or at least you may not have a job when you return.

"What? Camping?" Dean sputtered.

JP continued talking without acknowledging Dean's interruption. "I suggest you work together. I don't want any issues. I don't want any questions. I will be getting all your gear together, so be ready tomorrow. Yes, I said tomorrow. You two will be in a new wilderness. You *will* learn to work together for the survival of your job.

Are there any questions?"

"Yes, I have a question. Is there some other way you can teach us a lesson? I don't feel comfortable with this. This is not right! I don't want to camp, let alone with Dean," I blurted.

My mind was racing. *What is happening here? This is not professional. Where does JP get off making us work together in the wild? First of all, I did not poison Dean, and I'm being punished because Dean screwed up. I don't know anything about camping. But I can never let Dean know that I don't know; I can't give him the upper hand ever.* I had to keep all this to myself.

"Yes", I said, "I know you're getting our gear, but is there something else that we should bring? Such as clothing, a first aid kit, food?" Dean questioned.

Dean stayed calm, asking questions. I came off like the hysterical, outraged employee. I bet that was Dean's plan, he doesn't want this camping expedition as much as me, but he is not going to show it. I must keep my wits.

"I will provide all the gear and insect repellent for you. Yes, bring clothes, but I will supply some food since you will also eat from the land. I will have a book to show you what is edible and what isn't. Get your minds together and be ready tomorrow at 10:00 a.m. sharp to work as a team. I will send a text of the location If there are no more questions, you're dismissed. I hope you two don't fail. Goodbye, and happy camping."

Seriously, maybe coming to the Philly office was not a good idea, I thought. *There is way too many shenanigans happening here. I don't want to go camping with Mean Dean. This all seems odd. Please don't tell me JP is related to the CEO and his brother! Why would they come up with a camping assignment for us? This sucks.*

Dean responded, right away, "Thank you, JP, for the second chance. I will not let you down. I will be ready for camping tomorrow."

Dean and I walked out of JP's office. We looked at each other. He gave me a dirty look, and in return, I gave him a scowl right back. We parted ways as he marched off like a pouting brat walking in opposite directions.

I can't believe this is happening to me.

I was going to be in the wilderness, and JP didn't say how long I had to pack for. Oh my gosh, I desperately needed to talk to my girls. I had no clue how to survive in the forest, let alone with Dean Palmer. I knew one thing; I had to make this work because I wanted my job. I wanted to move to this new position, and I was going to show JP I am the right one for the position. I always rise to the occasion, and this will not be any different.

I am *a survivor, so Dean Palmer, get ready, you just met your match.*

DEAN

I couldn't believe this camping experience I was forced to have with the sexy schoolteacher. I couldn't believe JP thought that this was the answer to our screw-up. I was grateful I didn't get fired. The only thing I could do now was survive the wild with Crystal Harris. It was a good thing when I was a kid, I was a Boy Scout for a little bit. I guess I just had to tap into all those techniques I used back then. I was going to have to tell Brian about this.

On the drive home, I called him.

Hey Brian, you're not gonna believe this."

CHAPTER 8
Crystal

"Hey, Mom, are you home? I need to talk to you."

I walked into the living room and saw the television playing a Real Housewives show.

"Hey, dear, you're home early. Is everything ok?"

Mom walked out of the kitchen with her cooking apron around her, dusted with powder. Her pretty, long hair was wrapped up in a scarf to keep it out of her eyes while she baked.

"Yes, I'm fine. I wanted to tell you the outcome of the meeting with Mr. Pfeiffer. He's not firing Dean and me. Instead, he's forcing us to work together. He said that he wants us to go camping to force us to get along. If we don't work out there, then we won't stay employed."

"Oh, Crystal, that's awful. When will you be able to do your makeup and hair if you're camping, and why do you have to be with Dean? Is he a good-looking young man?"

Annoyed by her question, I answered, "I'm beyond caring about makeup and hair. Mom. It doesn't even matter that he is a good-looking, Korean man with a nice body and the face of a model. Too bad he's mean. His personality is just ugly and grumpy. Mr. Dean Palmer is 100% career driven. He is arrogant, conceited, and miserable."

I continued to tell her the more detailed aspects of what had happened at the meeting.

She stopped her baking. "Sounds like a match to me," Mom giggled. "Crystal, are you telling me some dogs were mating at your big meeting?" she gasped before almost losing her balance from laughing.

"Yes, Mom, I am," as I shook my head in disbelief, reliving that dreaded moment. "When will dinner be ready? I've gotta call my girls after the last few days I've had."

"Sweetheart, dinner will be ready in about forty minutes. Tell the girls I said hi and I miss them."

Before exiting the kitchen, I kissed my mom's right cheek. "Love you, Mom."

"Love you, Crystal."

I sent out a text in our group chat:

Hey ladies, I need you! 911. Advice is needed!

Mabel: What's up, Crystal? Ready now?

Chaundra: I am here

ME: Hello, ladies.

Chaundra: Heyyyy, Ladies! I've missed you, Crystal! I don't think Lelia is going to be able to make it.

Mabel: Heyyy! I miss you too! Crystal, you only live a few hours away. You need to visit more!

ME: I know I need to visit more. It has been so crazy since I came back from London. Now I am up for this big promotion. I'm so sorry, I'll do better.

Mabel: Ooo, a promotion?

Chaundra: I know London had to be amazing. What's this new opportunity you like?

ME: I am up for a senior executive position, but the issue is this guy, Dean Palmer, is also up for the position. JP told us that we both exhibit good qualities for the position. He said whoever wins the client will get the position. Now we are both competing. By the way, Dean is an ass.

Mabel: Senior exec? Wow, girl, you are moving up. I don't know who this Dean is, but he'd better watch his back. He doesn't have a chance.

ME: Thank you, girl, you always have my back.

Chaundra: These WCP leaders are no joke! J.P. is actually making you compete for the position? If he's like Hendrick Pfeiffer, then I'm honestly a little afraid for you.

I told my girls about what has been going on since I came home.

Mabel: Wait, the dogs were in the meeting? Noooooooo

Chaundra: Haaaa!! That is wild... I can't believe that happened!

Me: Yes, girl! The food was all over the room, it was a mess. Then the dogs started mating in the corner, ughhh. At the same time, Dean is doubled over in pain, and I think he shit his pants all in front of a client, and our boss.

Chaundra: "OMG... you're killing me! He actually crapped his pants?? I can't with this story!"

ME: I know it sounds hilarious, but at the time, it was devastating.

Mabel: Oh yes, I can imagine! I'm laughing now, but at the same time, I'm getting a chill in my spine just thinking about you watching your event be destroyed.

Chaundra: I mean.... Based on that alone, I'm giving you the promotion. At least you could control yourself.

ME: I had to control myself because I was so shocked I could hardly move. I could only stare in horror. The next day, the vice president told us he wanted to fire us, but instead, he spoke with the CEO, Mr. Hendrick, and Kendrick Pfeiffer, in your branch, Chaundra. I'm so embarrassed that our CEO now knows me primarily for the dog-humping incident instead of my work. So now we have to go camping together. He called it a "field expedition." Dean blames me for the failure of the meeting. He even said I poisoned him and made him sick.

Mabel: Oh, *please.*

Chaundra: Seriously? This Dean dude is blaming you? Now I want to kick his butt. I'm offended! Girl, watch your back. This is classic Pfeiffer shenanigans with this whole camping thing. They're so dramatic! What does JP think this is? Survivor or something?

Mabel: You need to document everything...I mean, you should be writing it down and taking video and audio, because this man clearly cannot be trusted, and this is not standard operating procedure outside WCP. I can't believe this shit flies...That said, I love camping, so I'm kind of jealous!

Me: Oh, you love it? Well, you can take my place.

Mabel: Nah, I can't fill your shoes, girl.

Me: I need your help, Mabel. I'm looking for advice on how to deal with Dean and how to survive camping. I haven't gone camping in years. JP said he will provide the gear, but I don't trust him. I am not going to lie, I am really nervous.

Mabel: Make sure you bring a good warm layer, ok? And extra socks, and some emergency snacks, ok? Do you have a small power block you can bring to charge your phone? What am I saying, maybe there won't be service...but you still need to record video and audio...and don't forget a lighter!

Me: Good thinking, Mabel. Thank you!

Chaundra: Well, you know the closest I get to the outdoors is Glamping. I need AC, running water, and maybe a mini-bar. Listen to our Wilderness Girl, Mabel. In my experience, you can't predict how these Pfeiffers are going to manipulate things. Please be on your toes. If JP is anything like his uncle, expect some sort of twist. I'll be honest, they're not normal!

Mabel: Definitely NOT normal. You need to alert your local union rep about this. Promise me you will send an email to your union rep before you go out on the 'expedition'.

Chaundra: ORGANIZE!!! LOL

Me: Mabel, I know you're the big-time union negotiator, but we are not all unionized. You're so funny! Thank you so much. You two are the best! I am so happy to have you in my life.

Mabel: Y'all need to get on that! Start a union!

Chaundra: Mabel, I don't think they have executive unions. Lol Not that we're not pro-Labor.

Mabel: Oh ok...well, whatever–talk to HR! This can't be on the down low! It's too weird!

My friends were really something else. Their support and comments were just what I needed. I was able to laugh at my predicament for a few minutes. They were the best!

Me: Good night, Ladies. Love you. Thanks again.

CHAPTER 9
Crystal

Day One

The next morning, I was at the assigned area exactly at 9:00 AM. I saw two backpacks and a note at the entrance of the heavily wooded park trail. I looked around, but Dean was nowhere to be found.

The note stated:

Here is your gear: stay warm and make sure you keep the insects off you. They are bad this time of year. Happy camping. There is more info inside your bags.

I would have thought Dean would have been here early since this team expedition is so important to us maintaining our jobs. I wasn't going to wait for him. Any chance I could get a leg up on him, I would take, since he was the reason we had to go camping.

I waited twenty minutes for Dean to show. I left him a note on the other backpack.

Dean: I am getting a head start. When you pick up your backpack, start on the path in front of you and catch up to me. Heading to the campsite.

I started on the path ahead and continued to walk for about forty minutes. I kept looking back, hoping to see Dean coming up behind me, but he was nowhere to be seen. I could hear the river, but I wasn't sure which direction the sound was coming from. I started to get nervous. Questions entered my mind.

What if there are animals that come out at night? I hope I don't see any wolves or bears. Oh no, I don't want to see any animals.

"Help, help me! " I screamed into the air. "Please, someone, help me, find me."

I began to walk toward what I thought was south. I started to hear something off in the distance. *Oh no, I'm delirious.*, I was hearing the woods call my name.

Is my mind playing tricks on me?

In the distance, I heard movement in the brush. Frightened, I looked around for a weapon. In high School I played softball, so I knew how to swing a stick with some oomph. I would look for a branch and use it as a weapon and swing on it. *Yeah, that's right, I got this. Mess with me if you want to, I've got something for you! I remembered people said there is a big foot, you can hear him but never see him. What if Bigfoot is following me?* My mind was swimming with wild ideas. I was starting to regret charging ahead without Dean.

I yelled with fake courage into the wild, "I hear you following me! You'd better get back, big foot or whoever you are. I will knock the fur off you!"

I spotted a large tree branch near my feet. I picked it up as if it were a baseball bat. I began to swing it wildly. The sound of ruffled leaves seemed to come closer. Whatever animal, or Bigfoot, that was coming my way would get hit so hard, it was going out park.

Momentary bravado aside, I nervously hid behind a large tree as I heard the sound coming closer to me. I could feel my heart beating faster and faster. *Is it a bear or Bigfoot? Is this how I go? Being eaten?* I won't go down without a fight!

I closed my eyes, listening as the sound came closer. Just as the animal or thing seemed to be on me, I came from my hiding position and began to swing widely with my eyes closed, screaming a warrior yell from the movie The Woman King. On the second swing, I made contact and heard a yelp sound. Terrified, I opened my eyes, and to my surprise, I made contact with a man on the ground holding his face.

Ready to hit him again, I bent over him still in shock, and growled, "Who are you?"

"What is wrong with you? Why did you hit me? You are *crazy*!"

The man turned to face me, rubbing his already bruised face, and I finally recognized him. It was Dean.

"Oh no, I am so sorry, Dean. I thought you were a wild animal or worse."

Groaning, as he rubbed his eye, he said, "I thought you were crazy, and now I know for a fact you are."

Ignoring his insult, I ran to help him sit up and look over his wounds. Getting a better look at his face, I must have hit him in the eye. I could see his eye was watering, and was slowly closing up. I felt awful, seeing the damage I caused. I didn't mind beating Dean at the office, but I don't want to ever physically hurt him, or anyone for that matter. *Why is it that when I get around this man, something out of the ordinary always happens? He thinks I poisoned him, and now he probably thinks I was going to bludgeon him with a tree branch.*

"Dean, I am so sorry. I swear I didn't mean to hit you. "

Looking up at me with his one good eye, he said, "Why would you think I was a grizzly, didn't you look? I knew I should have watched out for you, a psycho, sneaky woman that looks perfect and innocent all the time."

What did he just say to me? How dare he!

Defensively, I said, "Why did you sneak up on me? You could have been the psycho. You should have called my name to give me a warning."

"You wanted a warning? Well, that would have been easy if I knew your location. Please stop talking to me for a minute. My head is throbbing, and I think my eye is swelling up. I can hardly open it," he said exasperatedly.

I don't know why Dean thinks it is ok to call me names. I apologized. I hope he doesn't think I will tolerate him speaking to me disrespectfully. I am trying to calm down before I lose it and he gets hit in the other eye. After all, he should not have snuck up on me.

I took a deep breath to control my anger. I took my backpack and put it behind his head as he lay in the clearing in the brush.

He lay there holding his face.

After ten minutes, I approached him. "Hey, Dean, how are you feeling?"

"I am feeling better, I will get up in a minute," he muttered.

"No, stay there and rest."

"I never thought you would have gotten this far lost in the woods."

"Lost? I never said I was lost. I just wanted to get started camping right away. I was moving slow knowing you would catch up," I insisted.

Dean chuckled, "Sounds like you were trying to get a leg up on me and it backfired."

I ignored his comment.

"Dean, unless you know how to get out of here, I think we'd better prepare ourselves for the night," I said urged.

He immediately stood up and began to look around the woods. " I think we should get out of here." He started walking in different ways, trying to locate the path he had taken. Clearly frustrated, he looked at me and declared, "I'm lost! I don't know which way I came because you hit me, and I can't get my bearings. Thanks a lot, Ms. Harris!"

I was getting annoyed with his smart jabs toward me. "*Mr. Palmer,* I apologized. You know it was not intentional. What we are not going to do is continue to try to make me feel guilty for a mistake. I suggest you start being civil. Now, go towards the left, and you will find the path."

We walked to find a campsite. Lugging around the backpacks full of supplies JP provided for us was beginning to get heavy.

"I see a clearing, up ahead near the river, that might be a good location for us to start our campsite."

Dean nodded in agreement.

We both ventured toward the location.

Upon closer examination of the location, it appeared that this area had been used by other campers at one time. I could see where there was a makeshift fire pit, and the area was cleared out of shrubs and debris. I even noticed an area where someone had used natural elements to create seating with a log and a large boulder.

"Good eye, Crystal. This location looks like a good place to start camp. We can use the nearby water to find fish and wash our clothes and pots."

I smiled inwardly. Finally, I am getting positive responses from

Dean. I was getting sick of his sarcastic smart-ass comments, which he was constantly throwing my way.

We both threw our backpacks down. I explored our surroundings. It was beautiful here with the dense forest showing signs of autumn coming. The leaves of the trees were beginning to change red, yellow, and orange. The large rolling hills filled with those trees here in central Pennsylvania were breathtaking.

"Hey, I am going to look for wood for a fire before my eye swells up more, and Ionly have one to see with. Can you start looking through the bags for supplies?"

"Oh, okay," I stammered.

I guessed his comment was another dig. What did this guy want me to do? Fall to his feet and beg his forgiveness? No way, that was not going to happen.

Opening the contents of the bags, I began to lay it all out.

2 Pots

1 pan

1 compass

2 blankets

1 tent

1 Lighter

2 sleeping bags

Dehydrated meals

Energy bars

Trail mix

Insect repellent

Deodorant

sunscreens

Knife

Towel

Flashlights

Headlamp

First Aid camp

A note

I hope you enjoy your time camping. With this experience, I hope you learn to work together and learn that you have more in

common than you think. Now I'm giving you an assignment. I hope you didn't think you were going to have a camping vacation. On the other side of this paper, you will find a map. It has the location of your extraction. You will need to be there on your fifth day at 1300 hours, or you will have to find your own way home.

Happy camping,

JP

I turned the map over, and it revealed a map with a red flag. This was awful, not only was I forced to spend time with Dean, but we also had another assignment forcing us to work on. JP really has some nerve to make us stay out here, and for five days. I can't bear to think of spending one day with Mean Dean. JP thinks he is so clever punishing us like this. When I get back, I might have to speak to HR, because this is cruel and unnecessary punishment.

I was sure that somehow Dean would find a way to say this was my fault. He really had to start taking on some responsibility. Seriously, what was he, some angst-filled teen?

Wait, why is there only one tent?

Dean returned to the campsite.

"I was able to get some wood for the fire. Were you able to go through the bags? I'm going to need a lighter for the fire."

"Yeah, it's right here." I handed him the lighter.

He walked away to start working on the fire. I watched him struggling to get it.

"Do you need any help, Dean?"

"No."

"I think you need more than firewood." I tossed him a bottle of accelerant.

"Why didn't you give this to me from the beginning, Crystal? It would have been nice to have it."

"You didn't ask me for it."

He shook his head in obvious annoyance and went back to working on the fire.

I settled on setting up the tent. There were a number of rods and a lot of material. I was so grateful I spoke to Mabel before I came because she told me how to set up the tent.

Dean looked over and said, "Do you know what you're doing? I think we should move the tent further away from the water."

"Yes, I know how to put it together, and I'll set it further away."

Just about giving me another heart attack, Dean shouted, "Yes! We got fire!" Looking at him with his shorts on and a black t-shirt, he seemed so relaxed, almost pleasant. I was floored when he smiled a genuine smile, sweet and jovial. He had always been a handsome man, even with the constant attitude, but in this moment, with *that* smile, he was something else, something more. I guess being in nature really was good for him.

I threaded the rods through the tent frame. As I was setting up the tent, the wind came and blew it away toward the water.

"Ahh, the tent!"

I ran after it as fast as I could on the slippery terrain, but Dean ran right past me. He captured it from the cold water.

"Crystal, we gotta dry the tent. I am going to hang it up on a tree. I have bad news: tonight, we may be sleeping under the stars." He looked adorably remorseful as he delivered the news, soaking wet.

The thought of sleeping under the stars with no shelter wasn't exactly what I wanted to hear, but it could be worse. I guess it was a good time to give the note to Dean and let him know my bad news.

"In other news, JP gave us a note in the bag. He gave us an assignment." I handed him the now crumpled note.

Dean began to read it. His face seemed to morph with each line until—

"What? An extraction location! Five days! I can't spend a week in the woods with you, no offense."

"I *am* offended, but I feel the same way. I don't want to spend that much time with you, least of all *here*. Let's get through this. It is getting late. The sun is going down, and we don't have time for the tent to dry off. We need to find a good place for our sleeping conditions."

Dean nodded. We put our sleeping bags near a boulder overhang, which provided a little coverage. Our sleeping bags were about a yard away from each other. The fire gave us some heat and light, which was nice. We got settled and ate our granola bars that were provided. Given our exhaustion and surprise, we had little to say to each other. That was fine with me, though. I didn't need to spend time talking to the arrogant jerk.

There was nothing left to do. We both decided to get to sleep. The wind picked up, and the temperature fell. I was so cold, I trembled uncomfortably. I turned around to see how Dean was doing in this weather. He had his eyes closed, but I could tell he was cold too, his nose was turning red.

He opened his eyes and saw me looking at him. I immediately closed my eyes.

"Are you ok, Crystal?"

"I'm fine, just a little cold."

"Yeah, it is very cold and windy. I was hoping that fire would keep us warm. We can get warmer if we move closer to each other."

Is he getting fresh with me? I don't know if I should be closer to him.

"It's ok, Crystal. I don't want your teeth chattering to keep me up all night. Come move over here, and we'll put the blanket on both of us."

I got up and moved closer to him, wrapping the blanket around us. I lay down and he moved in close for us to spoon. Dean was right, the blanket over us made a big difference. I fell into a deep sleep and began dreaming of Spencer.

Walking into Spencer's penthouse, I saw roses on the floor leading to his bedroom. "Spencer, are you here? Where are you? Baby, where are you?" It was our 6-month anniversary. I knew Spencer had a surprise for me. He was just so loving and wanted to celebrate our love all the time. All of my friends told me that James was one of a kind because he was so into me and our love. Today he told me to come to his home because he wanted to have a special night with me.

Smiling a big old cheesy smile, I continued to walk towards his bedroom, noticing candles strategically throughout the living room. Walking into the bedroom, I see James standing next to the rose petal-covered bed in his shorts, smiling ear to ear.

'What is going on? This is so pretty, babe."

"Welcome, my love. I want you to know how happy I am that you have

allowed me to come into your life. Having you in my life makes me feel like all the pieces in my life now make sense."

Spencer took his hand to my chin and looked longingly in my eyes, "You're everything a man can want in a woman." He tenderly kissed my lips.

At that moment, I felt like nothing could take me from my high. That night, we made love in a way that was both desperate and fulfilling. Him, placing me on the bed and took his time removing my clothes, kissing my neck, moving down my body with kisses until he reached my kitty, and he tasted the nectar dripping from it. Seeing that I was primed and ready for him, Spencer adjusted himself, filling me up with all his manhood. Stretching my walls as they quivered with excitement.

He started with slow, long thrusts, and he began to go faster and deeper, until I called out and moaned loudly. The pleasure of intense throbbing was felt so strongly in my love button. With every rhythmic thrust, I screamed his name with the greatest pleasure. As the orgasm took me to uncontrollable heights, my body began to gyrate from shattering so hard. Spencer, Spencer, oh Spencer!

CHAPTER 10

Crystal

DAY TWO

I felt a hand on my arm shaking me.

"Crystal, Crystal, you up?"

I opened my eyes to see Dean looking down at me with a sort of perplexed, one could even say concerned, look.

Oh yeah, I'm really stuck in the forest with this man.

"What's up, Dean?"

"You were making some odd noises and moving around a lot like you were doing a dance choreographed by Michael Jackson with *a lot* of thrusts. I think you mentioned a person named Spencer. It looks like you were having a nightmare, dance routine, or an or..ga..sm." His eyes got big with the realization. The jerk laughed. "You were having a wet dream." He continued chuckling, looking at me with large eyes with that smug smirk on his perfect lips.

"What? NO! It was an absolute nightmare, I was running from a bad guy," I stated abruptly, as I got up swiftly from the sleeping bag and began to walk toward the creek.

Oh no, no! Please don't tell me I just had an orgasm in my sleep as I dreamed about that narcissistic man Spencer, of all people.

Dean must have heard me and felt how I was moving....

No! NO! This is the most embarrassing thing EVER!

How was I supposed to look at him again? Even worse, he already didn't like me. I'm sure he would tell everyone at WCP that I was having orgasms while sleeping next to him.

"I don't know what you think you heard or saw, but you know that didn't happen. I don't have time for you. I'm gonna go down to the water."

I marched toward the body of water near our camp. I just wanted to clean my face off and feel good after being in a sleeping bag without shelter. I felt so grimy, but I was even more annoyed with Dean teasing me. He always had to have something to say. I couldn't believe I actually had a wet dream, or at least it might have been one. Why was I dreaming about Spencer?

This is horrible.

When would I get this guy out of my head? The relationship has been over ever since I was in London. I had no desire to see him ever again. When we were together, it was hot and steamy, so I guess I couldn't escape that part of our relationship. I didn't want him. As a matter of fact, I didn't want *anyone.* I've been over men. I couldn't stand how every time I had a dream, it betrayed me by bringing Spencer into it. Now I had to deal with Dean for the next four days, teasing me about this. Even in my sleep, Spencer is trying to mess with my life.

I'm gonna act like nothing is wrong. I'm just gonna ignore him.

I got to the water and slowly dipped my hands in, then wiped my face clean. The water felt so fresh. It was cool, but not cold. I thought for a moment about how refreshing it would be to go for a swim for just a little bit.

Screw it!

I looked around for a nearby rock to put my clothes on. I noticed that Dean had wandered off from the campsite. I took off my shirt and my shorts and placed them there. I was so happy I listened to my mom and brought a bikini. I had the good sense to put it on underneath my clothes. I slowly walked all the way in, appreciating the refreshing touch of the water and the warmth of the sunrise on my face.

That moment in the water, I felt at peace—a peace I haven't felt since I started at the WCP Philadelphia branch. I'd been on edge. Dean and I, being in constant competition, had been stressed. He over-talked me in business meetings, and when I came up with ideas, he repeated them like they were his, which I noticed a lot of men do. I eventually started giving my ideas directly to JP before Dean had a chance to steal them.

It just seemed like if Dean and I were never going to get along with each other, that chance was long gone. Competition for the senior executive position destroyed any hope of that happening. It was funny, sometimes Dean was a total arrogant jerk, but at other times he seemed okay, as if there was something else buried beneath the work persona. His reputation in the office was a grump who never smiled, didn't date, and was all work/no play. I wondered if that was the true Dean. Maybe there was more to him.

I was enjoying the water. Diving under the water, I could see tiny, long fish swimming around me. Being in nature was truly wonderful and so relaxing. I started to do some backstrokes when I looked over to the campsite, and I saw Dean getting the tent off the tree. He folded it up nicely.

I guess it's time for me to go and help.

I didn't want to leave the lake because when I did, it would mean I had to face Dean, and honestly, that was the last thing I wanted to do. I got mesmerized by looking down into the water at a little black fish swimming around my feet. I smiled at the sight of it moving in and out, darting fast around my legs. It looked so free. I wished I could be as free as a fish, swimming at my own pace in life. Feeling courageous, I dared to venture deeper into the lake. The feeling was so invigorating and soothing that I stayed in the lake for another hour.

Deciding to get back to reality, I looked periodically for the looming eyes of Dean, but he was nowhere in sight. I headed back toward camp. I couldn't shake the feeling that something wasn't right. As I walked, I felt something slimy and cold on my arm. I looked down and saw that there were things attached to my skin. I screamed in terror as I tried to pull them off, but they wouldn't budge. Blood was running down my arms from pulling on the creatures. They were all over my body.

Dean, who was walking a few feet away, heard my screams and rushed to my aid.

"Dean, what is this? Help me, help me!" I cried as I stomped my legs, hoping they would fall off.

Dean

"Hold still, Crystal, I can help you if you stay still. You have leeches on you." I pulled over a sleeping bag and encouraged her to lie on it so I could help. "Here, lie down, I can get them off for you."

Trembling, she listened and lay down on the sleeping bag.

I examined the leeches and began to gently remove them from her arms, her legs, and her stomach. I continued to move them, making sure not to hurt her. As I worked, I looked into her eyes and saw the fear and pain that she was feeling. I knew that I had to do something to make her feel better.

I looked into her lovely eyes. "Don't worry, just close your eyes, I got you."

She closed her eyes and tried not to think about the blood-sucking monsters stuck to her luscious body. As I pulled the last leech off, I tried to give her some reassurance. "I'm almost done. You're doing great. Don't worry, I am on the last one."

She looked up with her doe-like eyes, so innocent and trusting. Damn, she is so beautiful.

"See, that wasn't so bad."

I took her hand and led her to a nearby stream. Crystal hesitated to go near another body of water. Couldn't say I blamed her.

"Don't worry, I was in here this morning, and there were no leeches. I wouldn't put you through that again, trust me." She looked deep into my eyes and nodded her head. *Yes, she trusts me.*

I washed her arms, long, toned legs, smooth, firm stomach, and round, firm butt, cupping the water with my hands and wiping the blood away from her warm mocha skin.

Damn. This is messed up, but Crystal is sexy as hell! How did I miss this?

I guess I was too consumed with getting the position to notice. Not to be a creep, but I was really enjoying wiping her down. Once I was done, I led her back over to the campsite. I turned over the sleeping bag and had her sit on it. I applied a bandage that I made by ripping my shirt to stop the blood running down her legs. As I worked on her, I gently whispered into her ear, "Everything is going to be okay. You're ok, beautiful."

Crystal looked up at me and smiled as she held my gaze.

In the sweetest voice, she whispered, "Thank you, Dean."

A warm feeling came over me as I watched her eyes flutter and then close. I'm guessing she passed out from stress or exhaustion. I covered her up with the blanket. I moved her wet, wavy hair from her face. Her beautiful, warm chestnut complexion against her wet, black waves made her look even more beautiful under the sunlight. *How is it that I never saw her in this way?* Brian said she was a hottie, but he said that about almost every woman. *I think we will be staying here one more day.* I wouldn't dare have her hike and walk after this ordeal.

She's had a crazy day. Our morning together started with me being awakened by her butt shaking on me. I wonder who she was thinking of? At the office, I never heard anything about her having a boyfriend. Wait, maybe she was dreaming of me, since we were in close contact, relying on each other for warmth. What I wouldn't do to be in her head, seeing her dreams. In the office, Crystal came off as a no-nonsense prude! She was attractive, but she acted like she wanted to have zero sex appeal. However, the way she moved on my back this morning... it was obvious she is more than a prude.

Crystal had me intrigued--she was a cunning, powerful businesswoman coming off prim and proper. She was having hot sexual dreams despite always wearing the most modest outfits, and now here she was in my arms, having passed out from seeing her own blood and all those leeches.

Something in me just wants to take care of Crystal despite our issues.

CHAPTER 11
Crystal

Day Three

I woke up in darkness. I was confused about the time. Was it night or was it early morning? I realized I was in the tent. The last thing I remembered was having leeches all over my body. I was petrified by all the blood that was everywhere. I closed my eyes in disgust. One minute, I was in the water swimming, and the next, I was covered in leeches. How did I get into the tent? I remembered Dean helping me, pulling the leeches off me. He was surprisingly really nice to me, not just nice, he was sweet.

Did he call me beautiful?

I had never known him to have a sweet bone in his body. I tried to remember how I got to be in the tent. I gradually remembered being carried. I felt like I was floating and I had opened my eyes to see Dean carrying me into the tent and placing me into the sleeping bag.

The tent opening unzipped, and Dean appeared in the moonlight, looking athletically muscular with his ripped abs, large, defined chest, and broad shoulders. It was *very* apparent he worked out—a lot.

"Are you awake, Crystal?" he asked quietly, trying not to disturb me if I was asleep.

"Hi, Dean. Yes, I am. Where were you?"

"I went to see if the blanket and sleeping bag were dry. It had blood all over it, so I put it in the stream to try to clean it. I wasn't able to get all the blood out of it. I was just coming back to check on you. I've been coming back to the tent every twenty minutes to see if you woke up."

"What time is it?"

"It's like three in the morning."

"Dean, when did you go to sleep? If I'm here, how did you sleep? I had the only sleeping bag."

He chuckled. "I didn't get to sleep. I was concerned about you. I wanted to keep an eye on you since the ordeal. I noticed the temperature drops at night, so I been attending to the fire."

I was shocked. Dean actually took care of me and looked out for me. I kinda felt bad he didn't get sleep, and it was pretty cold outside. I could feel the breeze coming through the opening in the tent.

"Thanks, Dean. I really appreciate you helping me. If you're tired, you can use this sleeping bag. I'll get out."

"No, Crystal, absolutely not. I will not have you get out of the sleeping bag for me."

"Come on, Dean, I don't mind. I am fine," I promised.

"No way, it's not going to happen. We aren't leaving this site until I know you are one hundred percent ok."

I felt there should be something I could do to make him more comfortable since he hadn't gotten to sleep.

"Alright, since you won't take the sleeping bag, come inside with me. I won't take no for an answer. Plus, we'll be warmer together."

I could see he was about to protest, so I looked at him and cocked one eyebrow at him. "I said I wouldn't take no for an answer." I opened one side of the sleeping bag and waved him in. When I opened the sleeping bag, I realized I was still in my bikini. I acted like I didn't care even though I did feel a bit exposed. "Come on, Dean, there's plenty of room. I know you're tired and cold. Thanks for keeping the fire going"

"I am, but only if you're sure."

He bent down and put his back to me as he layered the heavy cover over us. We both lay there in silence. Fifteen minutes later, I could hear

Dean's breathing go heavy. He had fallen asleep. I lay there feeling the warmth of his body next to mine. I moved my leg closer to him to feel his muscular hamstrings and calves. I gently placed my hand on his back after. The entire time, I was monitoring his breathing to make sure he didn't wake up. I moved my hand down his spine, and felt the firm muscles down both sides. I got even bolder and ventured toward his shoulders, and felt those muscles bulge. He was so alluring. I smiled in delight. *Damn, Dean is fine as hell.* I was lulled to sleep by the soft sounds of his breathing.

Dean

I woke up before Crystal. I could hear her rhythmic breathing and soft sighs intermittently between breaths. I turned around, she was still sleeping.

Lying next to her, I felt a little embarrassed that I treated her so badly. I thought about some of the things I said about her in the office, stuff like she was an awful businesswoman, she was cunning, and she wasn't qualified for the position.

I knew she was aware of the things I said about her. At the time, I didn't care if she knew how he felt. I wanted her to hurt like I was hurt. Guess the saying was true: hurt people hurt people. I looked over at Crystal, and I saw her waking up. She really was a beautiful woman with her warm, dark complexion, long, thick hair, long lashes that complemented her dark eyes, thick, pouty lips, and a sprinkle of brown freckles that fell under each eye. I wished I could have taken back some of the words.

"Good morning, Crystal," I said softly. She didn't move. I put my hand on her shoulder and lightly shook her. "Time to wake up."

Crystal slowly opened her eyes before moving to look over her body. She glanced over the remains of blood on her ankles, legs, and stomach with repulsion, then what seemed like relief.

"Thank you again, Dean, for helping me. Seeing the leeches sucking on me was so disgusting."

"Yeah, well, I kept trying to wake you, but you were really sleeping hard. Are you thirsty or hungry? I can get some water and oatmeal for you?"

Crystal

Dean got up before I could answer and ran off to find me water.

I actually could hear him trying to wake me, but I just pretended I was still asleep. I was a little embarrassed that he might have noticed that I felt him up before I went to sleep. I decided to act dazed and confused. From what he said, he was tired and slept hard. Hopefully, he didn't realize I was feeling up his sexy back.

I was humiliated that Dean had to take care of me. He probably thought that I was so weak. I hated to look weak in front of him, after all, we are business rivals. Sitting up and trying to wipe the blood off, I thought more about the last two days together. *Did I hear that right?* He called me beautiful. *Does he think I am beautiful?* Shaking the thought away, I realized he must be making fun of me because I knew I was far from beautiful in that moment.

Dean came back with a refilled water bottle of water from the natural spring he found and handed it to me.

"So how are you feeling, Sleeping Beauty. Leeches like standing water, please use the stream for now on?" He smiled sweetly.

Sleeping Beauty. Why is he being so nice? This was the same guy who couldn't look at me at work because I pissed him off by wanting the same position. The same guy who ruined my relationship with our new client with his friend's dog. I coughed and looked up at him.

"Thanks, Dean, this is exactly what I needed. I'm really dehydrated."

I gulped down the water as he kept his sexy, dark eyes on me with a grin. *Why does he have to smile at me like that?* He looked so handsome and tan. The sun was making him a stunning golden tan. He was tall, dark, and handsome. *What am I thinking? His looks are irrelevant.* I had to stop thinking about his beautiful body and the way he looked when he was studying me while he was cleaning me off.

I remembered seeing in his eyes, concern and... lust. *Dirty Boy... No, no, stop thinking like that.* I was just happy I didn't have another wet dream with him last night. Even more grateful Spencer didn't invade my dreams again. *I gotta get away from him.*

"Hey, I am going to stretch my legs for a bit. I'm going to go get some more water from the spring and wipe this remaining blood off me. Thank you again for the water." I said cheerfully.

I stepped out of the tent with Dean behind me. I swiftly walked off, grabbing a shirt and putting it on.

Dean

I watched Crystal walk away. What a sight she was, walking away in her bikini bottom with my t-shirt on. I started to think that maybe she was embarrassed about passing out from the leeches since she seemed to be upset about being freaked out. Leeches were disgusting, so I couldn't blame her. I decided to make a fire. Oddly, when people on TV made a fire, it was really fast and easy. In reality, it wasn't easy, and definitely not fast. I used a stick to poke at the fire, hoping to get some burning embers.

I didn't mind taking care of Crystal. It felt nice to make sure she was good. She looked like a sun-kissed Sleeping Beauty. I could never have looked at her sleeping until this situation. She really was stunning to look at. *I think she likes me.* Last night I felt her touching my back, maybe she was dreaming. She was a very active dreamer. It felt nice having her touch me, and I didn't want her to stop. I just pretended to be sleeping. I almost broke out in a snore, but then I thought that was going too far, so I kept rhythmic breathing. There was something about this woman, she was vulnerable and strong, but at the same time sweet. I didn't know, she made me feel weird inside—like I wanted to show her I could be nice and caring.. a better man.

Crystal

While in the spring, I decided to get some twigs. I wanted to at least try to do my part to help out. I was grateful Dean looked out for me. I just didn't know how to take him. *Was he this nice guy now?*

Walking back to camp with an armful of sticks and twigs, I noticed that Dean wasn't there. I guess he went to do some exploring. *Thank goodness.* I felt so relieved. I still wasn't ready to see him after my little grope session this morning. To keep my mind busy, I held up two twigs. I wanted to start a fire like I had seen Dean do a few times. I did not know the location of the accelerant, so I began to rub the twigs together faster and faster. It seemed like nothing was happening. I didn't want to have to depend on Dean for everything. It was bad enough that he saved me from the leeches, and I fainted. *Mabel, where are you when I need you?* I laughed.

I'm NOT a weak woman. I can take care of myself! I snatched up another pair of twigs and rubbed them together, fast and faster. Still nothing, so I touched the area on the twig where I had been rubbing it, and it felt hot. *Yes! I must be on the right course.* I kept rubbing. I broke my concentration when I heard a voice behind me laugh.

I turned around to see Dean looking down at me with a charming grin. He had taken off his t-shirt and used it to gather something. Looking at him, I couldn't bring myself to say anything because I was trying to keep my jaw off the floor. I was stunned by his lean, muscular chest. *This man screams sex appeal.*

"What are you doing?" he asked between his laughs.

"What does it look like?" I said sarcastically. "I'm trying to start a fire."

"I see." He grinned. "Well, let me show you. It will be good for you to know in case something happens and I can't do it."

I started to roll my eyes. Dean really knew it all. I was doing fine making the fire. I was sure that if I just had more time, I would have been a success. Patience was one thing I had in abundance. I had been patiently dealing with him in the office, being rude to me and challenging my every move.

He went through all the steps to build a fire and gave multiple scenarios if one technique didn't work.

"Oh, thank you for sharing that information. It will be very helpful. I hope one day I can get my *skillz* up to par," I retorted with a hint of sarcasm. "Who would have known you're a super nerd when it comes to making fires and surviving in the wilderness," I teased with a smirk on my face.

Dean returned the sarcasm, "You're welcome, School Teacher. It is good to know you appreciate my *skillz,*" he mocked as he kept working the fire into a large flame.

"How would you feel about making some food over the fire tonight? It's late, and we'll be at this site until tomorrow morning," he said optimistically.

I couldn't help but smile at his cheerful tone. "Sounds like a good idea."

CHAPTER 12
Dean

Day Three - Nightfall

I found some rice and canned beans in our WCP survival kit. I began to make the rice first by boiling a bottle of water and putting one cup of rice in the pot. The beans would be a lot faster. I would put them on the fire when the rice was done.

"So while we wait for the food to finish, tell me something about you, Crystal?"

Looking confused, Crystal asked, "What do you mean? Maybe you should ask me directly what you would like to know. Or are you asking me to get some dirt on me for the gossip hounds at work?"

Chuckling, I said, "That's fair. I will ask you a straight question. Ok, so tell me how come you look so damn perfect all the time at work. You dress so conservatively, and it seems you never put your hair down. I mean, you are excellent at what you do, but you seem like there's another side to you that you won't let anyone see. It's perplexing."

"Wow, Dean, that was not what I was expecting you to ask me. Well, if you're asking me questions, you better be open to me asking you questions as well."

Yes, ma'am. I nodded, "Yes, after all that would only be fair."

"I was raised in a very conservative household in West Chester,

Pennsylvania. So dressing conservatively has always been me. I just feel most comfortable dressing like that. Honestly, I am supposed to hook up with my girlfriend Lelia's designer to give myself a new look," she laughed. "I had a traditional household. My mom and dad only had me, so I was the center of attention until my dad left us. I was about twelve years old and a daddy's girl. I loved him so much. In my mind, he was the most handsome and funniest man in the world when I was a kid."

She told me more about what happened to her parents. Her father sounded awful. How could he have done that to her? I could imagine little Crystal, so cute with two pig tails, sitting on her Dad's lap, smiling while her father sings his little song to her. Then, in another vision, I see her calling for her daddy, but he just walks away from her, never returns to her life. If he wasn't her father, I would kick his ass. How dare he hurt her?

She continued. "The loss of my dad was upsetting, but I have a wonderful mother who supports me in every way. She went to London with me during my internship. She takes care of what is most precious to me. My mom is always encouraging me to let loose, but I want to be as perfect as I can so that I know I'll be successful. She worries about me all the time. She just wants me to enjoy life.

Does that answer your question, Dean?"

Grinning at this incredible woman, I answered her. "Yes, it does, thanks for sharing that with me. I'm sorry about your dad." She was perfect. She was in the wilderness, looking sexier than I ever seen her before, with her hair flowing freely and a little bit more relaxed. She had just seemed to blossom right before my eyes.

"Ok, my turn, Dean. At the office, you come off as a person that people can't get close to. You don't want to make relationships with people. You're all about business and building your career. You never smile, and you're not mean, but you don't come off as a nice guy. You seem to want to win, and anyone who's in your way had better watch out. What's your story back? It seems like you had a traditional upbringing. I can see you as a little kid making campfires with your dad. Oh, by the way, move the rice from the fire so it doesn't get mushy."

I moved the pot out of the fire as she instructed.

"Ok, good observation. Yes, I am career-driven. I do want to make relationships with people, but I'm not good at it. I just fail whenever I try. I don't know if you heard, but I had a work friend who turned into my girlfriend. Her name was Zara. I was in love with Zara, but I don't think she was ever in love with me. I gave her my heart, and she cheated on me when I went home to take care of my father. I was ready to propose, but she had found someone more successful. I was devastated because I didn't see it coming. So after that, I just focused on my career. So I guess your assessment of me is *almost* correct."

Crystal looked deep into my eyes; hers were filled with concern.

"I'm so sorry to hear about your relationship with Zara. In my opinion, she didn't deserve you, Dean. What was wrong with your Dad?" she inquired.

I took a deep breath because talking about my father always gave me anxiety.

"I grew up in Wilkes-Barre, in a modest upbringing. My family was not poor. We were your typical blue-collar household. I grew up with my parents and my two brothers. My father worked at a factory that produced lawn fertilizer. He was an average father, he worked, hung out at the bar with his friends after work, and came home to have dinner with the family. My mom was a stay-at-home mom. Things were pretty normal, except for my father being obsessed with me playing sports." I stirred the rice as I contemplated how to say the next part.

"I was a disappointment to him. See, when I was young, my dad always spent time with me. He would put me in every sport and come to all my games. Having him at all my games was a nightmare. He would yell at me during the entire game, and if I didn't work hard enough for him or my skills were not up to what he thought they should be, he would make me practice after the game for hours. All while yelling at me, *'It's in your genes to be a sports superstar, you are not working hard enough.'* Which was odd for him to say, since he was a mediocre athlete in high school, according to my mother. He told me I was his golden ticket and I had the makings to be a star."

"That sounds like he was trying to live his dream through you. That's a lot of pressure, Dean."

"Yeah, I was happy he thought so highly of me, but the price was not worth the yelling and overworking. One time when I was seventeen, our basketball team made it to the national finals. We won by one point, but my father didn't like the fact that I didn't rack up most of the points, and the point spread wasn't wider. To punish me, he made me do practice shots in the dark all night in our yard. I passed out from dehydration. The next morning, my mom was so upset when she found me outside on the ground. She got me in the house and told me that I never had to play sports again if I didn't want to. I heard my parents yelling. My father said that I cost him a bet and he lost a lot of money. He was punishing me because he bet on me."

I just shook my head, thinking back at that time, with disgust. "I don't know what she said to my dad, but Mom put her foot down. Finally, I was done! Ever since I stopped doing sports, he never liked me."

I looked up, and Crystal's eyes had tears shining in them as she hung on to every word. Her beautiful face showed she sincerely cared about what I was saying. Her hands were clasped tightly together.

I continued with my story. "He stopped talking to me and had no time. To this day, he says I could have been pro. He and I don't get along at all. The odd thing is, I have two brothers, and he doesn't treat them the same way he treats me. One doesn't do any sports, and the other is a mediocre athlete. My mother is beautiful, she is a very strong, five-foot Korean woman, and she loves her sons. I don't know what she saw in a redneck white man like my dad. They are complete opposites; she is sophisticated, and he likes drinking beer excessively and hunting with his friends. I can say, if it weren't for her strong will, I wouldn't be the man I am today. She's always positive and supports me no matter what. I love her so much. I went out to my parents' home when my father was diagnosed with cancer. I returned home to my girlfriend, loving another dude. There you go, Crys, that's my sob story."

Changing the conversation, I pointed to the fire. "Hey, it's time for the beans."

CRYSTAL

I had no idea that Dean had it so bad growing up. His dad was an ass. I cut the silence. "Wow, your dad is a rough guy. But your mother sounds like a gem. I don't think these fathers know what they do to their children. I doubt they even care." I said, shaking my head.

"I know I will *not* be the man my father was to my son or daughter. I will have the same drive you see in me at the office and more for my children and family." Dean said with a set determination in his eyes.

At that moment, Dean really turned me on. I knew the timing was off but the fact that he was so determined to be a good father was so attractive.

Dean walked over to the beans and gave me a bowl of rice. I tasted the duo, and it was delicious. I was so hungry, I hadn't eaten since the day before. We both began to eat our dinner. For a few moments, there was just the sounds of nature, animals, and insects filling our ears.

"Dean, this is delicious, thank you for this dinner, and everything else. You really came through for me."

"Crys, it was not a big deal. I was happy to help. I felt bad for you. You were in the water, enjoying yourself, and then leeches were all over you. It was a rough ordeal. It probably was best that you fainted, and didn't have to deal with the worst of it."

I chuckled to myself, amused that he called me Crys for the second time. The only person who ever called me Crys is Lelia. For some reason, he reminded me of her. Maybe it was the Korean connection since she was Black and Korean. Although Dean had a white father, they both had loving Korean mothers.

"I am grateful," I said, smiling and looking at him as the moonlight illuminated all his best features, which were all of him. His thick black wavy hair, strong chiseled jaw, high cheekbones, and deep dark eyes, which I kept finding myself getting lost in more and more. I couldn't pull myself away from his smile, it was so bright that it made me feel warm from head to toe.

Clearing his throat, Dean asked, "So who's Spencer, the man you were dreaming about?"

I stared at him for a moment, but figured I'd come clean since he did. "Ahh, yeah, I'll give you the short version," I sighed. "When I was in London, my boss, who was a Vice President of the WCP London office, asked me out. We dated and became a couple. For no good reason, he broke it off after eighteen months of dating. No reason, just left me heartbroken. I left WCP London to come to the Philly branch. I never spoke to him again. I think because we never got closure, memories of him enter my dreams. Hopefully that will come to an end soon," I said matter-of-factly.

I felt good telling my story with no emotion. Up until that moment, I hadn't been able to talk about Spencer without getting emotional. *I think I had a breakthrough. Yes!*

I looked over at Dean, who had a major pissed off look on his face.

"What's the matter, Dean? You look pissed."

"I hate hearing that this guy, Spencer, had your heart and didn't cherish it or you. To leave you with no explanation is so immature. A real man would never treat you like he did. He didn't deserve you," he said emphatically.

Wait, Dean is seriously pissed hearing my story about Spencer. I loved how he championed me. It was becoming very hard not to be attracted to this man. I knew I said no more men, but Dean Palmer was really making me second-guess my decision. This man was really checking all my boxes.

"I agree, Spencer was immature and so hurtful. I'm better now than when I first came to Philly. Believe it or not, WCP really helped me. It gave me something to do and think about. I was tired of wondering why Spencer didn't love me, why I wasn't worth staying for? I kept being reminded that was what my mother felt when my dad left us, and making me even more miserable."

Dean moved closer to me on the log until his natural scent mesmerized me. He gazed at me, "Crystal, don't feel bad, I think you're an amazing woman. You gave me a run for my money at work. Not only are you a good executive, but you're a kind and strong person who deserves to be loved."

He was even closer now, and I could hear my heart beating in my chest.

"Crys, I hope this doesn't make you feel weird, but I find you irresistible. That Spencer guy was a fool."

"He was?" I murmured. Somehow, our faces kept drawing closer to each other. It was as if a magnetic field was causing us to connect. Our noses touched.

"Umm, I really need to kiss you. May I?" he said in a seductive whisper.

Yeees, Yes, Yes! Now I was fully turned on. There was some major throbbing happening in my girly regions. I hadn't kissed a man in almost a year. *I am going to kiss Dean.* This hot ass man was about an inch away from my lips, asking me questions. I wanted to say, *Yes, you silly man, kiss me before I kiss you.* It was so considerate of him to ask, though.

"Yes.. you can kiss me... Dean." I smiled while the butterflies in my stomach threatened to make me say something else.

Dean leaned forward, and his warm lips finally touched mine. As soon as his lips touched me, it felt like a jolt of electric chills went through me. His lips fit perfectly on mine. I put my hands around the back of his head while I balanced my weight on the log. Dean placed a hand around my waist while his other hand caressed the left side of my face, and slowly slipped into my hair. I opened my mouth so I could taste him and let him know I wanted more. Dean got the hint and parted his lips, taking the lead with his tongue by placing it deep in my mouth. Our tongues were doing a sensual dance as our mouths became one. In between kisses, he whispered, "Crystal, you're so enchanting."

He took his arm that was around my waist and picked me up. I quickly wrapped my arms around his neck and my legs around his waist. Dean carried me to the tent. We feverishly kissed each other the whole way. Once he gently laid me down, we caught our breaths and stared into each other's eyes.

I tried not to fall for this man, but damn, there was something about him. Now I couldn't get enough of him. Breaking our longing stares, I kissed him tenderly and ran my hands through the soft waves of his hair.

CHAPTER 13
Dean

Day Four

W*hat am I doing?* I knew I had feelings for Crystal, but what was about to happen between us? I wasn't sure if this was right. She was my arch nemesis at work. We were in competition for the same job. I couldn't forget how dirty she played me, getting me sick. *Okay, that might be a bit harsh.* To be honest with myself, I was a little scared.

I pulled back from Crystal. I instantly saw the confusion in her eyes.

"Crystal, I don't know about this. What are we doing? I need some time to think. I'm so sorry." I got out of the tent and went for a walk along the water line.

I really like Crystal. Wait.. I really do like Crystal. I would love to see where this could go. I was man enough to admit I was afraid to put my heart on the line again. I didn't want to punish Crystal for what I went through with Zara. They were so different. Zara was so concerned about what others thought of her. She would never let anyone know her background if it wasn't perfect. Crystal opened up her childhood to me and the bad relationship she had in London at WCP. Crystal is just a more real and honest person. The concern I saw on her face when I told her about my father showed she was compassionate. Unlike Zara, she hated to hear about anyone's problems. I remember her saying, "I *don't like to hear about people's sad stories, it's giving poor."* I was so disgusted with her comment. Overall, Crystal was a much better person; she had many of the attributes I saw in my mother. No wonder I admired Crystal.

CRYSTAL

What just happened with Dean? One moment we were hot and heavy, and the next minute he was second-guessing himself. *He isn't sure?* This situation resembled the problem I had with Spencer...a lot. He just changed up for no reason, just like him. He was outside walking around, and it was about to get dark. *I am so done with men.* They were so scared of everything when it came to relationships.

Stepping out of the tent, I noticed the fire was getting low. I threw some nearby twigs on it to keep it going while he was walking around, trying not to be scared. *Ha!* I was just so exhausted. His heart seemed to be off course, out of nowhere. I didn't have time for him to get himself right. *Damn, I hate Dean Palmer!* He was the same guy I knew from the office. Why did I think he could change? I went to collect water at the spring nearby. I saw Dean on the bank, stooping down, throwing pebbles in the water. He looked like he was really torn and trying to make a serious decision. *Who cares about Dean and his decision?* I walked over to the spring and got my water filled. He stopped tossing pebbles in the water when he saw me. I think he thought I was going to be like, *What's wrong, Dean? Can we talk?*

Nope! I don't care, and I will not *be speaking to him.*

I filled my bottle and walked away without a word. I walked back to my tent, got one of my books, and fell asleep reading it. Dreaming.

Looking down at Spencer, I saw his head going between my legs. I felt so excited. When he put his wet, slippery tongue on my girly region, I felt like I was going to scream in pleasure.. He hit my spot, and an uncontrollable feeling came over me. I succumbed to the pleasure of it.

When his head came up wet from my juices, he spoke in that deep voice, "Beauty, turn over on your stomach."

Feeling very obedient in his company, I followed directions. He placed his hand under my stomach and encouraged me into doggy position. He then stood up and positioned himself behind me. Spencer pushed his manhood into me, filling me entirely. Slow, easy thrusts became faster and more powerful. We moved in rhythm until he came. Exhausted, he collapsed next to me in the bed. He kissed me and fell asleep. I lay in the bed listening to him breathe. Questioning if sleeping with Spencer was a good decision. Eventually, I fell asleep alongside him.

When I woke up, I didn't see Dean. I knew he fell asleep next to me in the tent, but he didn't get in the sleeping bag. I was only aware of that fact because I was freezing last night. When I got out of the tent, I saw him. I asked him to get wood for the fire since it was out. He shrugged and walked away.

I went to the nearby spring to wash up and put on a fresh pair of shorts and a top. Walking back to the camp, I saw Dean chopping wood. I guess he was hot from chopping for some time because he took a water bottle and poured it on his face and chest. *He looked incredibly sexy*. In an attempt to bring things back to normal between Dean and I, I tried to strike up some kind of conversation. I came behind him and patted him on the back lightly while friendly calling his name.

Dean immediately turned around to stop chopping the wood. While looking at me over his shoulder, he asked, "What did you say, Crystal?"

"I was saying you go, Dean. You're doing a good job. That's all," I said brightly.

"Crystal Harris, I don't need your approval for doing a *good job*." He made quotation marks with his fingers. "I definitely didn't need the approval of a person who cheats at work."

Wow... He must be crazy. Who does he think he is speaking to? He must have me twisted with someone else.

Looking up at Dean, I narrowed my eyes on him.

"Dean, don't take your insecure issues with intimacy out on me. We had a moment, and you got scared and ran. I get it if you are not sure about your emotional feelings; it is ok, because honestly, I'm questioning my actions with you. You will not start accusing me of cheating and using false accusations as a way to hide from your feelings. Don't come at me sideways because you can't handle being an adult. You're just another immature man. Dean Palmer, grow up!" I shouted.

With those words, he widened his eyes in surprise and walked away from me.

I watched Dean walk away into the forest. I hoped he would use that time to think about what I said to him. I guess it was up to me to find wood. The fire was just about out. He was walking off like some spoiled brat. I could honestly say I couldn't stand Dean Palmer. I hated how he was cool one moment and ice the next. Who could deal with someone like that?

Sighing, I walked away from Dean towards the opposite side of the forest.

I started to walk deeper into the woods to collect more twigs and placed them into a canvas bag. I couldn't wait to go back to the office. I wouldn't speak to him unless I had to. I hated his mood swings. He kept calling me a cheater? He had some nerve! I hated his whiny attitude. I spotted some berries near a prickly bush. *Yay! Something other than rice and beans.* Reaching for the blackberries, I got my hair stuck. Man, why did I have to even bother trying to get these black berries?

After getting unstuck and being able to stand up straight, I had prickly flowers all in my hair. I tried to pull them out. I could imagine what Dean was going to say when he saw me. I could just hear Dean The Downer say, "Oh, look at the schoolteacher with her messed-up hair. It's definitely an improvement," just like a little boy. Then again what did I care what he said about me? I shouldn't even be thinking about him. An image of Dean's handsome face came into my mind with his disapproving look.

Focus, Crystal.

Collecting the rest of the sticks and twigs, I headed back to the camp, pulling and tugging on my hair. On the path back, my sneaker hit a rock, and I fell. I dropped the blackberries, and the wood fell to the ground. Frustrated, I got up, brushing off the dirt and leaves off my clothes. I noticed a feeling of liquid running down my leg. I looked down for a closer look. My knee had a huge gash that was leaking blood down my leg. It was worse than I expected. I was already feeling defeated this morning. Why not add physical pain and possible infection to the list?

I bent down and brushed the dirt away from the wound. I was startled by loud shouting.

"Ahhhhha Ahhhhaha."

I looked up, and I saw Dean running to*ward me,* yelling at me while banging two of our cooking pots together. I was in shock at the scene for a while. Looking in his eye, I started to think, *Oh no! I'm in the woods with a madman.* I was freaked out. Was Dean a killer? Has he lost his mind? He was coming at me with pots and wild eyes .

Oh my gosh, I'm gonna brace for impact. I think he's going to hit me. Is he out of his mind?

"Dean, what are you doing?" I screamed with fright.

"Crystal, I need you to turn around slowly, but don't run," he yelled as he continued to run toward me.

Following his directions, I turned around slowly. In front of me was a large, and I mean giant, black bear standing on all four legs, looking at me. My heart jumped, and my eyes could have rolled out of my head from the sight of the bear. I took a deep breath, but it seemed like I forgot how to breathe. My heart was beating too fast. Dean caught up with where I was standing. He got in front of me and put his arms above his head, both hands holding our camping pots, which he banged together. He was still between the bear and me.

Everything was moving so fast. I was so scared I couldn't move. My body felt like my legs had weight on them, and if I were to take a step, I wouldn't go anywhere. The big black bear stood up on its two hind legs and roared at Dean and me. Dean, still standing between me and the bear and me, roared back with a heavy, loud voice, with the clanging of the pots growing louder in the background. The bear dropped down on all four legs again, turned around, and ran away from us. Dean kept slamming the pots, harder and harder, until the bear was out of sight.

"OH SHIT," I said, still stunned with terror.

Dean turned around, looking at me with panic, fear, and surprisingly, concern in his eyes. Taking both of his hands and placing them on both sides of my face, he spoke.

"Crystal, are you OK?" His voice was gentle but urgent like he desperately needed an answer. His eyes searched my face for an answer I was still too shocked to speak.

He saved me again.

After a second, I was finally able to stammer a response. "I'm fine, thank you for saving me. I can't believe you did that!"

I turned my face toward his chest, and we both wrapped our arms around each other in a tight grip, realizing how close we both were to dying. I could feel Dean's chin on my head. We must have stood there feeling our heavy hearts beating together for what felt like an hour. Treasuring each other and the lives we still had.

Dean tenderly pulling back to look down at me into my tear filled eyes, he asked again, "Crystal, are you oK? I was at the camp straightening up and cleaning our pots when I decided to look for you. I thought I saw you but you disappeared."

"Yeah, I fell." I said, shaking in his arms.

"I guess you did because when I looked back to find you, I saw you were facing the camp and bending over."

Dean, pulled me closer before holding me tightly. "Crystal, while you were bent over, I saw the bear skulking toward you." He moved the hair out of my face as his eyes burned into mine. We stayed in that moment, allowing our unspoken words to pass freely.

Tears were fully rolling down my face now. "I was brushing off the dirt off my knee, see." I backed away a little to give him a better view of my angry wound.

"Thank you so much for saving me, Dean. I don't want to think what could've happened if you didn't show up and save me.. again."

Dean pulled me closer to his chest, I could feel his heart beating fast.

I felt so much more secure and safe in his arms, and he was just so brave to get between the bear and me.

Smiling down at me, he said, with his deep voice full of certainty, "Crystal, I wasn't going to let anything happen to you. Let's go back to the camp."

Walking back to our campsite with my arms crossed around my middle and Dean's strong arms around my waist, he led me over to the makeshift chair that consisted of a log in a boulder. He sat next to me, moved his arm up to my shoulders, and rubbed my arm in comfort.

"You're alright, Crystal. The bear is gone. I think he was just as scared as we were," he chuckled nervously.

"I agree, but I think he was just scared of you. Your quick thinking really came in handy. How did you know what to do?"

"I saw it on television. I think it might have been on one of those survival shows in the wilderness. I really don't remember. I knew I should make myself larger and make as much noise as possible. I'm so happy it worked," he laughed. "More importantly, you didn't get hurt."

"I am fine, just a little shaken up. I am grateful for your swift action, Dean."

"As long as I'm around, I'll never let anything hurt you," he said, all joking, leaving his voice entirely.

He is really giving off knight in shining armor vibes ... I can work with that

"You stay here, I am going to get the rest of the wood after all, it is my fault you were getting the wood in the first place. Here's my Yeti mug with fresh water. Take a few sips, and calm your nerves. I know I was being an ass earlier, and I'm sorry for that. Stay here. I won't go too far. I'll keep an eye on you, Crys."

I must have looked a fright. While he went to get wood, I decided I was going to try to clean up my knee and fix my hair in the stream.

I care how I look. I want to look good for Dean. Why do I care?

CHAPTER 14
Dean

My heart was still pounding from the bear situation. I had to look calm for Crystal's sake. I felt bad for leaving her in the tent. I could have lost her forever, because I was too scared to put my heart on the line. Of course, I could have smashed and moved on, but not with Crystal. She was a different type of woman. I have feelings for her.

Yes, I. like Crystal Harris. I'm going to let her know. Damn, I am so attracted to her.

I was done with being afraid of getting my heart hurt. I was more afraid of never experiencing love again, especially with someone as incredible as Crystal. I hurried to get more wood and headed back to the campsite. I had to make up with Crystal.

"Hey, Crystal. I'm back," I yelled.

I heard a splash, and I saw her washing her wound on her knee. I waved to her. She smiled that brilliant smile and started coming back to camp.

"Dean, I'll be right back. I had to wash the dirt from my knee and get these weeds out of my hair. She replied.

What a sight! Her dark, slicked-back hair cascaded down her back and shoulders as water dripped from it. Her white bikini accented her beautiful brown skin. Her tits were magnificent; they looked like two melons ready for my appetite and pleasure. Her hips were wide enough to create that perfect hourglass shape. Every step showed off her thick, firm thighs. This woman was stacked. Every time I saw her, I found myself having an uncontrollable desire for her.

She walked toward me. When she got closer, I saw concern on her face.

"What's going on, Dean? Why are you looking at me like that? Did you see the bear again?" she whispered, concern lacing her voice. She scanned the forest with her eyes.

Holding myself back from running toward her, I responded, "No, but I want to tell you something important."

Grabbing a towel from the log she placed there earlier, she wrapped her luscious body in the towel. She walked up to me, searching my face for answers.

"Were you going to tell me it's about to rain? I can tell the clouds are getting darker. I felt a few raindrops when I was washing up in the stream. I figured if I were near the water, I would be safer there than at the tent. Less likely a bear will go into the water for me," she chuckled.

"No, that's not it."

"Oh, what is it?" she asked inquisitively.

Feeling inspired to take a risk on us and be real about my feelings.

Crystal

I wasn't sure what was up with Dean; he had a wild look in his eyes.

"I don't want to play it safe, allowing my heart to go off course, away from you."

Before I could reply, Dean pulled me toward him. With lust in his eyes, he kissed me. This time, his kiss was not slow and sweet. This kiss was passionate, affirming. It was deep, long, and claiming. Taken by surprise, it took me a few seconds to realize what was happening. I kissed him back, matching his intensity.

Raindrops began to fall around us.

Dean's hands wandered all over my body as he continued to kiss me, letting me feel all his passion and desire. He explored my back, my waist, my butt, and my breasts so delicately, like he didn't want to miss a single inch of me.

Our breathing was getting heavy and more desperate. As I began to explore his body, I felt the muscular curvature of his smooth chest. I noticed his nipples were as hard as mine, so I grabbed one and squeezed it teasingly, making him give a low groan. He grabbed my bikini top between the cups and pulled it off.

Without any hesitation, Dean picked me up by my waist, and I wrapped my legs around his middle. His lips discovered my nipples. His mouth captured my breast, sucking and licking my nipples. A small yelp of pleasure and pain escaped my mouth from the intensity of his sucking. My bikini bottoms were wet from my lust. The intense throbbing between my legs had me hungry for Dean's dick.

"Take me," I whispered in his ear.

Reacting to my words. He stopped kissing my breasts and moved to my lips. He carried me to the open sleeping bag that was just outside the tent. The rain was coming down on both of us, but we didn't care; Dean and I had unfinished business to take care of. It was going to happen, now, in the rain, in the wild, for all the animals to witness our primal lust. There would be no hesitation, no second-guessing. We would have all our desires met.

He lifted me gently onto the sleeping bag. Dean looked down at me and gazed for a moment.

"You are perfection," he exclaimed

I started to pull at his shorts, desperate to feel him. He assisted me by pulling them off. He took his mouth and bit one side of the strap of the bikini bottom, and began to pull off my bottoms with his teeth. Now we were both naked. For a moment, I took in the sight of his large dick. It was beautiful! A beautiful shade of light tan, about eight inches in length, with a slight bend to the left. I felt my pussy react to seeing it.

Dean brought his attention back to the matter at hand. We hungrily began to kiss each other. He moved down to suck my neck. I knew he was leaving love bruises, and I couldn't care less. The animal in me came out as I moaned loudly in pleasure!

I ran my hands through his wet, black, wavy hair as he feasted on my neck, my shoulders. I moved my head to the side to give him more access. *He can have all of me.* "Yes, Dean, yes, yes!" I screamed.

I rolled on top, looking down at him as I took a more dominant position. Being here with him like this brought out these aggressive, lustful feelings, and they took over me. Raising my bottom to position my dripping pussy over his eager dick, I lowered myself down his shaft. My pussy was taking it in slowly. Once fully inside, I braced myself to ride him like I'd been wanting to. I rode him like he was a stallion, and we had a finish line to get to.

Dean's eyes were closed, but his panting turned into loud groans. I couldn't keep quiet. I released my moans of a sensual pleasure that I never felt before. Bending over as my ass went up and down with perfect rhythm with his pelvis, I whispered in his ear, "How you like this juicy pussy, Dean?"

I could see his eyes go back into his head from complete pleasure.

"Crystal, you don't know what you're doing, talking to me like that. YES! YES! I love your tight, juicy pussy. It's sooo good!"

Hearing his reply made me ride that stallion harder and faster. We screamed loudly, and a feral roar escaped our mouths as we reached our climax.

Dean sat up and wrapped his arms around me. We both continued to roar loudly as our orgasmic pleasures reached their height, never stopping our perfectly synced rhythm until our last primal yowls were made together. At that moment, we were one with nature. We didn't care who or what saw us in the wild. This was real passion, raw lust at its finest. We didn't give a damn about anything right now. Creatures great and small could come look at the pair of us getting our groove on. Look and see our lust! This was how real hunching was done!

In our embrace, we both shivered in each other's arms, but not from the pouring rain that relentlessly fell upon us. We shivered in each other's arms because of the high intensity of the orgasm. It took a while for our bodies to recover. We held each other silently and tenderly.

Dean broke the silence, "Crystal, that was incredible. I have never experienced sex like that. You're ..."

I put my lips on his lips and kissed him.

"I know.. words can't express it.. right? It was on another level," I said softly.

We just sat there for a moment looking at each other, holding on to the moment.

"Let's get out of the rain and go in the tent and dry off."

We walked with our arms around each other's waist to the tent. Once inside, Dean took a towel and began drying off my body. I did the same for him. We lay down next to each other, exhausted from the day's activities, and fell asleep in each other's arms.

I feel myself falling for Dean... easily.

CHAPTER 15
Dean

Day Five

I woke up with the biggest smile on my face. As I opened my eyes, I found Crystal nestled comfortably in my arms. Watching her sleep, she appeared so peaceful and serene. The calm of the morning air filled the tent as I inhaled deeply, allowing myself for a moment to reflect on the incredible love session we had shared.

Throughout my adult life, I have had my fair share of partners, yet I have never experienced anything as intense as the night before. Crystal's confidence and the way she took control, climbing on top of me with assurance, left me speechless. My attraction to her goes beyond the physical; I am deeply intrigued to get to know more about this fascinating woman.

As my eyes fell on a sleeping Crystal, I gazed at her beauty. I wondered if she was dreaming of me. I couldn't help but notice the strength she exudes. Crystal was a woman unafraid to put me in my place and call me out on my boyish actions. She truly was a sexy ass boss. I decided I was going to get her some berries for her oatmeal this morning. We would have to get to the retrieval location soon. Gently, I bent down and kissed her cheek.

Crystal

I woke up alone again. I would have to have a talk with Dean about leaving me sleep late. Last night with Dean was breathtaking. I felt so close to him.

Something came over me when he kissed me. I felt like I was floating. Who would have known Dean was a great kisser? I didn't expect us to sleep together, but when you're in a dangerous situation, people tend to cling to each other. Seeing how brave Dean was, saving me from the bear, turned me on. I lost control and wanted him so badly. I was hoping he didn't have regret—I was worried he ran off because he didn't want to face me.

I realized that I probably looked wild from last night's activities. I went through the bag and pulled out a brush, a hair tie, and pulled my hair back in a high ponytail and let two wavy ringlets fall on both sides of my face. I found a fresh bikini and a pair of jean shorts. I walked to the spring to wash up and brush my teeth. Dean had really changed the way I looked at him. I was really catching some strong feelings. I couldn't stop smiling, thinking of him, as I was leaving the tent.

I saw Dean on my way to the spring. He walked up to me and asked possessively, "Where do you think you're going?" before he bent down to give me a kiss.

Blushing with a big smile, I answered, "I'm just going to the spring to wash up."

"Ok, don't take too long, I have a surprise for you," he said with a grin.

"Ok, I won't," I promised with a smile.

"By the way, I love your hair," he said as he walked away.

I washed up fast in the spring, eager to get back to Dean and the surprise he had for me. I couldn't believe I was out here trusting another man.

I hope he doesn't break my heart. I have to have faith. Dean truly is different. He is special.

After washing up, I went back to the tent. Inside, Dean was waiting for me. On a towel, he had put berries that he picked in the shape of a heart, next to a cup of oatmeal in a Yeti bowl.

"Come here, Crys, I want to tell you something."

I sat down in front of him.

"I was done with love, and I wasn't gonna allow anyone in my heart again until I met you. I thought we would be enemies at the office, but you stole my heart. I had my heart on the course of loneliness. I don't want to be lonely at night. I want you in my life, filling my days with your beautiful smile and filling my nights with your love. Will you consider dating me exclusively?"

"Dean," I found myself blushing as I spoke. "I must admit, I didn't see a love connection with you. I was done with men. You've stolen my heart, and now I am on course to falling for you. I would be honored to date you exclusively. *My Hero*"

We leaned over and shared a tender kiss.

I think we needed each other. It felt healing

CHAPTER 16
Crystal

"Dean, this is the last day. We need to get to the extraction point in a few hours. I can't believe I'm saying this, but this was the best experience I've ever had. I kinda hate to see it come to an end." I gushed.

"Crystal, I agree we need to go to the extraction point. It has been really amazing being just us together with no distractions. I really fell for you hard, Miss Crystal Harris! If we could stay here in the forest, just you and me, I would be so satisfied. Oh yeah, I gotta include the bear and leeches," he chuckled. Leaning over me and kissing my forehead.

We began to start packing up our gear. Once we were just about packed up, Dean got the map out to see how long a trek we had.

"So, Crystal, it looks like we don't have to go too far. We have about three miles uphill, and it will be a clearing at the top of the mountain. I am going to walk ahead and look at the terrain. I will be back in ten minutes to get you. Stay here and make sure we have everything packed up. Ok, babe," Dean said

"Okay, don't be too long, you know I am going to miss my *hero,*" I flirtatiously teased.

Dean left with his backpack to check out the terrain. I finished packing our backpacks. With time to spare, I began to look for two walking sticks for both of us. I sat on the log we used to sit on when we talked around the fire. Reflecting on our conversations, Dean and I have a lot in common. We both have been hurt in love, and our salvation was our loving mothers. Both of our fathers disappointed us. I was so happy we had this time to get to know each other. If we weren't stuck on this camping expedition, we might still be at each other's throats.

Looking down at my watch, I noticed twenty minutes had passed and Dean, aka my hero, had not returned. I walked over to the area where he walked off. I didn't see him walking back towards camp. I didn't want to worry, I took a deep breath and decided to wait ten more minutes. In the ten minutes of waiting, my mind began to run wild with thoughts. Maybe the bigfoot dude is real, and they are chilling together. Maybe the bear came back, and he is defending himself.

When thirty minutes passed. I decided to get my backpack on, get my walking stick and go look for him. I noticed that the terrain got more rocky as I took the steps up the mountain. After walking for ten minutes, I stopped and looked around. This should have been the point at which he should have turned around to come back to me. I decided to call out his name.

"Hey, Dean Where are you? Dean, Dean!"

I received no answer back. Feeling very concerned and nervous for him. I looked up at the sky, according to the sun, we had about three hours before it began to set. It was imperative that I find him. I began to reflect on what Mabel taught me and the books I read about camping. I continued to walk up the trail. I could tell this could have been the way he had gone by the fresh broken branches, low to the ground.

I finally found a good guy, but I lost him already. How does this happen to me?

Hiking up the trail, I noticed a black shirt or cloth in the field.

I shouted, "Dean, Dean Is that you? Dean? Dean!"

"Crystal, it's me come over here, but be careful of the rocks in the field."

Relieved and so excited, I found him. "Don't worry, Dean, I am coming," I sighed.

I am coming to get my man.

When I reached him, I noticed that he was sitting with a distressed look on his face. *"Dean,* what is wrong? Why didn't you come back to me? Are you hurt? I fired off questions to him, trying to understand the situation.

"Babe, I was hiking up this hill when I saw some beautiful flowers in the clearing. I wanted to return to you with a bouquet of flowers. So, I walked over to get them when my boot got caught in a hole, and I tripped. When I tried to pull my foot out, a large rock got dislodged and fell on my ankle. In this position, I was unable to move it."

Looking closer to inspect the scene, there was a mini boulder that had fallen on his ankle. The size of the huge rock must weigh hundreds of pounds. His ankle was in a position that looked very uncomfortable.

"Dean, I am going to move it off you. When I tell you to move, pull your body back with your arms. I don't think you will be able to move your leg, okay?"

Dean nodded his head in understanding.

I took my walking stick and pushed it under the large rock to get leverage on it. Once I got the stick lodged well under the rock, I turned to Dean.

"Okay, Dean, when you see me use my walking stick to raise the rock, I need you slide back. Can you do that?

"Yes," Dean said in discomfort.

I moved my stick up, and the rock began to move off his ankle. I noticed Dean followed my directions exactly. He slid back as fast as he could. As soon as his ankle was clear, I dropped my stick in relief because it was a struggle to hold up and rock up.

I immediately went to Dean. "Are you okay, Dean? Let me see your ankle."

Dean leaned over to kiss me on the cheek and handed me the bouquet of wildflowers he picked.

"Aww, thank you, babe, they are beautiful. After all this, you still got me flowers? You are so sweet," I gushed. "How is your ankle? I'm so concerned for you. Can you move it?"

"I can move it, Crys, but I am not going to lie, it really hurts," Dean whimpered.

I very gently tightened his laces on the boot. I did not want to take off the boot and run the risk of swelling. We would not be able to put his boot back on due to swelling. "So Dean, I don't know if your bone is broken or sprained. I think the best thing we should do is keep the boot on and put a makeshift splint on it to minimize movement."

I immediately found a stick to use as a splint. I then went into my backpack and pulled out my white bikini tops and used them to tie around his boot and ankle.

"Thank you, Crystal, for helping me. How did you know how to do this first aid stuff? I'm truly impressed by you," he said, admiration overriding the pain in his voice.

I kissed him on the lips. "I don't know. It all just clicked in my head. I know stability is key when there is a potential break. I am just happy I went looking for you and found you." I reassured him.

We sat together for ten minutes with our arms around each other, enjoying the moment in silence.

"Crystal honey l, I can try to keep walking to the extraction point."

" No, Dean, that will not happen. I want you to relax. When it's time, I will go to the extraction point and get help for you. We have time. Let's just sit here for a moment and rest if you are ok with that."

Dean nodded, in agreement.

I lay my head in his lap, and he stroked my hair. My adrenaline surge to help Dean made me exhausted. I slowly fell asleep.

I had to save my man. Make sure he is good.

TWO HOURS LATER

I felt a hand on my shoulder shaking me. He roused me out of my sleep. I looked up at Dean. "What's up? Are you ok, Dean?"

"Yes, I am fine. I dozed off too, but I heard something. I wanted to wake you."

Frightened, I said, "Is it a bear?"

"No, No not at all. It was a human, like someone talking," he consoled me.

I exhaled in relief. Wait, I did hear something.

Far away, I could hear someone calling a name. I pulled away from Dean.

"Do you hear that?

"What?",

"Stay here, let me look." I stood up to get a better look at our surroundings.

I saw two figures walking towards us.

"Hey, Crystal and Dean is that you?" the pair yelled at us.

I waved at them. As they got closer, I was able to recognize Sophia and Brian.

Excited to see both of them, I called for Sophia. "Sophia over here!"

Sophia's eyes located me, and a large smile appeared on her face as she walked towards me. Ever the fashionista, she was dressed in a camouflage top and shorts, a pink bandanna, and a pink belt. She looked beautiful. Sophia and I ran toward each other and gave each other a big hug. We were so happy to see each other.

Brian bent down and gave Dean a handshake and a hug. They were both talking to each other about how happy they were to see each other.

Sophia pulled me into a second long hug.

"I am so happy to see you two. Dean is injured. What's going on? Why did you guys come out here looking for us, and how did you find us?" I said excitedly.

"Well, Bryan and I wanted to find you because we had something we wanted to tell you first. The way we found you was that Mr. JP put an AirTag in your bag, so we had an idea of your location."

Of course he did. I should have known JP wouldn't risk the liability for his little experiment.

"Also, we have a confession..." Sophia trailed off.

"Confess? What would you have to confess to us?" Dean asked.

"I want you to know we feel awful that you two had to come out here and were punished together in the woods, camping and trying to survive with lions and tigers and bears," Brian said, laughing.

"No, but seriously, we did feel bad. We need to confess that one of the reasons why you're out here is because it's our fault. We feel awful about it." Sophia interjected.

"Bro, I'm so sorry I brought Max to the presentation. I know you didn't really know 100% that I was bringing him. I know I mentioned it, but you never really gave me permission to bring him, and it was my fault that the whole presentation was a failure. I mean, you were doing a great job. The aftermath was really my fault. Sorry, Dean. Sorry, Crystal." Brian had enough sense to look ashamed as he made his confession.

Sophia cleared her throat. "Crystal, I also have to make a confession. The day we had the tea with Mr. Russell, Dean came in late. Well, Dean, you came in, and you were kind of surprised that we were there having tea and having a nice chat with Mr. Russell. You demanded to have some tea. I want to let you know I gave you tea, but it wasn't the tea that everyone else was drinking. This tea was called Smooth Smooth. It was a laxative tea. I take it sometimes when I cleanse my system. I know I shouldn't have done it, but that's why your stomach was so messed up. I feel absolutely awful. Crystal didn't know anything about this, so I'm really sorry, Dean. It was really all my fault. We had to confess to JP. We felt it was only right that we find you guys and bring you back to the office. JP is not upset with you two. He told us to come get you. He *is* a little annoyed with us, but I think we'll survive."

Dean and I just stared at them for a moment. Then Dean and I looked at each other in surprise.

"All this time I thought Crystal had given me something to make me sick, and it was you, Sophia, all along."

"I thought Dean sabotaged me by bringing Max the dog. Now I found out it was you, Brian."

Sophia and Bryan looked so remorseful.

Dean and I said in unison, "Thanks for confessing. It's okay, we forgive you, too."

Dean and I smiled at one another. They may have screwed up, but we gained so much more thanks to their mistakes.

"Help me up and get my backpack so we can go home and take a proper shower," Dean said.

"No problem, Dean, thank you for forgiving us," Bryan said with a smile.

Sophia hugged me and said, "Thank you, girl, I love you."

"Yeah. Dean, you can really use a shower. What have you been doing? Sleeping with the bears?" Brian asked, laughing.

We laughed and packed up to head home.

CHAPTER 17

Crystal

The next day, I went to my office to review my emails, most importantly to see if I got an email from Mr. Russell. As I reviewed my emails, I separated the junk mail from the priority mail. There was a knock at my door. It was Sophia.

"Good morning, Crystal. I'm happy you got settled in. I want to review a few things. One, you have a meeting with Mr. JP, later this morning around 11 o'clock. Also, there is a very fine-looking man in the lobby requesting you."

"A man?" I questioned, "Do you have his name?"

"No, I don't have his name. I can tell you he's about 6 feet tall, gorgeous, muscular, and is asking for Crystal," Sophia said with a big grin.

I was confused about who this person could be requesting to see me. I exited my office and headed toward the lobby. As I walked to the lobby, I saw Trey. This was odd. Why would he be here? As I got closer to him, he noticed me, and a big smile appeared on his face.

"Crystal, I'm so happy to see you. I was so worried, I wanted to make sure you were ok. He bent down and gave me a long hug."

Surprised by his declaration and hug, I rattled off my immediate questions. "What do you mean you're worried about me? Why would you be worried about me?"

Trey released me from the hug and looked down at me. "I know you and I have standing appointments, and I noticed that you missed three appointments, no call, no show, and I know that wasn't like you. I was really concerned. I was just walking by the building, and I said to myself, 'This is where Crystal works. Let me come inside to see if I can find her."

"Oh, I'm sorry I missed my appointments. I had a last-minute work engagement that took me away from the office, and I didn't have a cell phone," I said apologetically.

"Ok, I was very concerned after some of the conversations that we had. I wasn't sure what could've happened, but I just wanted to make sure you were alright," Trey said happily

"Thank you, Trey. I appreciate that. That means a lot that you care enough to come down here to check on me. I'll set up another appointment soon. I just came back from camping, and my back really aches from lying on the ground," I said, rubbing my back.

"Ok, sounds good. Contact the receptionist and make an appointment as long as you're good. I'm good. I will see you soon. Stay positive and be open to all the good and love you deserve," Trey smiled and gave me one last hug.

"Thank you, Trey." Out of the corner of my eye, I think I saw Dean watching us near the elevator as I was released from the hug. I turned my head, and the elevator door was closed. Where did he go? Was he on the elevator? Was he watching me hug Trey? I hope he was ok and didn't get the wrong impression. I decided I'd give him a call later.

I walked Trey out and said my goodbyes.

I pulled out my cell phone to call Dean. The call went straight to voicemail. That's odd. I wonder why he would have his call forwarded to voicemail.

I returned to my desk. But I couldn't stop thinking about the night before with Dean. He was so darn sexy. The way he touched and handled my body.

Sophia stuck her head in my office. "Crystal, are you ready? Mr. JP would like to see you now."

"Ok, I'll be right there. Do you know if Dean will be joining me in this conversation with JP?"

"No, not that I know of. He just asked me to get you, so if you're ready, I won't leave him waiting."

"Ok, I will be right there," I said nervously.

Reaching into my desk, I took out a mirror to make sure my hair was in place. I decided to wear it down in its natural spirals, although my mother protested against me wearing my natural curls this morning. I was determined to love myself. Not what other people expected of me. I added some extra gloss to my fully defined lips and kissed myself. I looked great.

Straightening out my black pants and salmon colored top. I walked to JP's office.

Seeing his assistant wasn't present, I took the liberty of knocking on the door.

"Come in," a voice behind the door uttered.

As I opened the door, JP was sitting at his desk.

"Crystal, come take a seat, please."

"Hello, Mr. JP," I said as I took my seat.

"How did you like camping?"

"I really enjoyed it. I learned a lot, and I think I'm ready to really work as a team and bring in more clients."

"That is good to hear. I was hoping that you and Dean would find some things in common and be able to grow from what you learned from each other. Were you able to do that?"

"Yes, Mr. JP, we were. I think we learned a lot about each other—actually, I know we learned a lot about each other, and as a matter of fact, I found out that we have more in common than I ever expected, so it was a great idea for you to put us together. I believe we both have a newfound respect for each other, and the shenanigans that happened before will never happen again."

"That is good to hear. I was so disappointed in how the meeting turned out with Liam, but I'm happy to say that everything was saved, and he was still very impressed with you. He felt that you really understood the product. You understood him and his needs. He said that you were a great fit to work with him and the new product. With that being said, Crystal, you have earned the new position. You are now the new senior executive director of marketing affairs," JP said happily.

"Really? Wow...I mean, that's...I'm honored, but why did you end up picking me over Dean? He also worked really hard." I was feeling this weird mix of emotions, because of course I wanted the job, but now I also wanted Dean to share in the position. We really had come to understand each other out there in the woods. Our working relationship was about to be amazing.

"Now, don't worry about Dean, I have something special for him, and he'll be very happy. I'll let him tell you all about it. So go ahead and celebrate your promotion and know that I see you both as senior executives."

The biggest smile appeared on my face. This was the position I had been waiting for, and now it all seemed like it was going to work out for both of us.

"I'm so excited. I'm so happy, thank you, Mr. JP. I will not let you down. I really appreciate this opportunity, and trust me, you will not regret your decision. Thank you so much."

"Well, you earned it, Crystal. The London office told me that you were a force to reckon with, and you are. You deserve this position, and I'm really looking forward to working together. You also get a new office. Go celebrate and get ready to move up to the sixth floor."

I stood up, shook JP's hand, and walked back to my office. I saw Sophia looking up at me with a questioning look.

"Come to my office, Sophia," I said, trying to contain my excitement.

She came in and closed the door behind her.

"Guess what, Sophia, I got the position."

We both squealed in delight. "Oh, I'm so happy." We literally jumped up and down in our high heels.

"I am so happy, you deserve it."

"Thank you, Sophia."

"I will need an administrative assistant. Would like the job?

"Are you serious? I'm going to be an executive assistant!"

"Yes, if you accept the position."

Yes, yes, yes, absolutely!. Oh, I'm thrilled."

"Great, we're moving on up to the big office on the sixth floor.

We're moving on up!" We sang in the manner of the television show, The Jeffersons' melody.

"Sophia, have you heard from Dean? Or have you seen him? I tried to call him, but it went straight to voicemail. I wanna have a talk with him to see how he feels about me getting the position."

"I saw him. I didn't know why, but he was upset about something. I saw him and Brian speaking, and he had his phone in his hand. The last thing I saw was him leaving the lobby. His face was very rigid."

"I'm going to try to call him again now." I picked up my phone and dialed his number. "The call went straight to voicemail again."

I decided to text him.

When you get this message, give me a call. I hope you're well. I was hoping to talk to you soon.

"Hopefully, he'll call me back. I hope he's not upset with me for getting the position. I mean, he knew one of us would have to get it. Also, JP said he had something special for him. Maybe he was upset he saw me hugging Trey," I said, thinking about it a little more.

"Don't worry about it, Crystal. When it comes to Dean, we never know what's on his mind. His face looking rigid is kind of normal sometimes, but he did seem like he was a little bit more serious than usual, and that's saying a lot for Dean because he's pretty much no nonsense, no fun at all."

"Ok, thank you, Sophia. I'm just gonna finish my emails, and then I think I'm gonna work from home."

"Ok, sounds good, Senior Executive of Marketing, Crystal Harris." Sophia laughed.

I laughed, too, when I noticed she put emphasis on the Senior executive.

Although, I was laughing on the outside, I was really upset on the inside. I couldn't stop thinking about Dean. *Why is Dean not answering my call?* I thought we had a major breakthrough last night. I wonder if he is upset because he saw me hugging Trey. Oh no, what if he thinks I'm just like Zara, ready to cheat on him at any free moment? I grabbed my laptop, put it in my bag, and started walking to the elevator to go home to see my mother.

After I briefly spoke to my mom, I ran up the stairs to my room and closed the door behind me. I looked through my WCP contacts to look for Brian's number.

"Hello."

"Hi Brian, this is Crystal. How are you?"

"Hi, Crystal, I'm fine. I thought you were somebody else. What can I do for you?"

"I've been trying to reach Dean, and I've been unsuccessful. I was wondering, do you know where he is or is there something going on with him?"

"Crystal, I wish I could help you. The only thing I know is that he is on his way back to his parents' home. I don't know why. He didn't go into detail. All he said to me was that he's going back home."

"Thank you, Brian. If you hear anything else, please let me know."

"Will do, Crystal. Take care."

Dean was going back home to his parents' house. Oh no, this might be worse than what I thought. I remember hearing that when he found out about Zara, he left for a couple of days to his parents' home. Oh no, he must think I'm talking to Trey. I need to contact the girls to get advice on this one.

ME- 911 I need helpful advice. Dean and I had a romantic encounter in the wilderness, and we did it. Long story short, big misunderstanding with my massage therapist, and now Dean's ghosting me. He's going back to parents, like he did when his last girlfriend cheated on him. What should I do?

Lelia- Hi, Crystal, I can talk. I see you have a major issue. Tell me more.

Me- Dean and I made a strong connection. When we returned to WCP, I was awarded a position that we were both in the running for. Not to mention the other guy he saw me hug. Now he is going back to his parents' home.

Lelia- What is the last name of Dean?

Me- Palmer.

Lelia-LOL.

Me- What is so funny?

Lelia- That is my cousin. His mother is my aunt, Bomi Palmer. He is from Scranton, right?

Me- Wow, what a coincidence, you're his cousin. But he is not from Scranton.

Lelia- Oh, yeah, that's right, they moved to a new house a few years back. Dean is a really good guy. I am sure he is not upset with you getting the promotion. To make you feel better, I'll text you his address. If you want to go see him. He is a romantic, so I hope he doesn't think you are interested in another guy. I don't like the fact that he's not calling you back. Do you want me to call my aunt?

Me- No, don't add his mother in this. Send me the address, I am going to see him. Thank you, Lelia, love you!

Lelia- Go get your man, Crystal. LOL Love you too, bye!

Throwing my phone down onto the bed scanning my room from left to right. I could feel my heart beating like I just ran a mile. I'm gonna take my relationship into my own hands and tell my side of what happened. As I went through the closet pulling out outfits just in case I decided to go to a hotel, since after all, the drive was three and a half hours long. I heard a knock at the door of my bedroom before it slightly opened.

"Dear, are you ok? I hear you talking to yourself like you're a cheerleader, hyping yourself up," Mom giggled.

"Yes, Mom, I decided to go to Scranton, I mean Wilkes- Barre to see why Dean isn't answering my calls. I know I sounded like a cheerleader, but I kinda had to talk myself into this because I was really feeling unsure. I know it is rash, but this scenario is a reminder of Spencer and me. I don't feel very comfortable not having answers. I'm packing for an overnight trip just in case I stay, and I'll contact you when I get to Wilkes-Barre."

"I agree with you. You need answers, and it's nice to see you take charge of your situation. I wish I had done the same with your father," she said as she looked down. "Maybe I would've been in a different place in my life."

"I love you, Mom. You are the most loving person I know, and I am better off as a person because I've had you as my mother." I walked closer and gave her a kiss on her cheek, bringing back her smile.

I was exhausted from the day. I wanted to be fully alert while going up North, so I decided I was going to go eat lunch and get on the road. My mom agreed--she gave me a kiss and walked out of my room.

"I love you, Crystal," she said.

"I love you too, Mom," I replied back.

CHAPTER 18

Crystal

"Mom, I'm almost at Dean's parents' house. I tried to call him, but still no answer. I am getting a little nervous, Mom." I said while on the phone with my mother, driving.

"Now, Crystal, don't second-guess your decision," she said. "You got this!"

"Thanks, Mom. I'll call you later." I just needed a little reassurance.

Arriving at Dean's parents' home, I pulled up to the two-story brick colonial with black shutters and a red door. I noticed the perfect landscaping. I took a deep breath. I wasn't sure what I was going to say when I got to the door. I noticed the dark clouds moving in. I figured it would rain soon. I opened the door of the car and began to walk up to the front door. I put on a bright smile and knocked at the door.

I heard a voice behind the door saying, "Hold on a moment." The voice sounded like it came from a middle-aged woman. A moment later, the door opened with her saying, "I apologize, Zara. I was just finishing... I'm sorry you're not Zara." The petite woman said, "Please accept my apologies. How can I help you, dear?"

Dean is here with Zara? Why did she mention her name?

"Oh, are you here for Dean?"

"Yes, I'm here for Dean."

"Well, come on in, dear. It's going to rain soon."

As I followed her into the kitchen, I noticed several flower bouquets in the living room, accompanied by cards.

"Take a seat, and I'll make you some tea."

"Thank you."

I really couldn't say anything else, because I wasn't sure what was happening. I came here to see Dean, and he seemed not to be around, but his nice mother invited me into the house. She was expecting Dean's ex-girlfriend, Zara, but now I was about to have tea with his mother. I was a bit confused.

"What is your name, dear?" She placed a small pink China tea cup in front of me.

"Oh, I'm so sorry. I'm Crystal Harris. I work with Dean."

"Well, it is a pleasure meeting you, Crystal. Call me Bombi, and I am Dean's mother. Thank you for coming to my home. I don't often get a chance to meet Dean's coworkers. Sorry to call you, Zara. She is supposed to stop by."

"It's a pleasure to meet you."

"Dean stepped out. He should be back soon. It is so nice for you to be here for Dean at this time. His father passed away a few days ago and it was very sudden. I couldn't get hold of Dean for days. His phone kept going straight to voicemail."

Oh no! While Dean and I were on the camping assignment, his father was dying. No wonder there were so many flowers and cards in the living room.

"That's so terrible...I guess he told you we were on a work trip and out of cell service."

"Yes, I understand about that now. When I couldn't reach Dean, I reached out to Zara to help me find him. That's why I thought you were Zara when you knocked on the door," his mom revealed.

Oh it makes sense now why Zara was here. I felt a lot better about that part, anyway.

"I'm so happy I met you, Crystal," Mrs. Palmer smiled as she poured the tea into our cups.

Returning her smile, "I'm happy to meet you, too. I am so sorry to hear about your husband's passing away. If I had known, I would've bought your family flowers," I said sympathetically.

"Oh no, Crystal, no need. I have so many flowers already. It's just nice to have you as a company. Dean's father was sick, but you're never prepared for someone dying. We all knew that it was going to happen eventually, but nonetheless, it's a shock when it happens. Michael Palmer didn't always get along with Dean, but one thing I know is that Dean loved his father and wanted his father to be proud of him. As a child, I never saw a child who looked up to his father so much, seeking his approval. None of Dean's brothers cared to get Michael's approval--they might be a bit of mama's boys." She chuckled.

She began to weep. " I can't believe my husband is dead," she sobbed. Slowly, I saw tears fall down her face as she gazed into her cup of tea.

I felt so bad for her, and I got up out of my seat and put my arm around her to comfort her. Her sobbing was interrupted by a knock at the door, taking a nearby napkin from the table. Mrs. Palmer began to wipe her tears away.

"Thank you for comforting me. You are a darling. Now, who is that at the door?"

"Would you like me to get the door?"

"No, dear, you stay right here. I'll be right back," as she patted me on the back, walking by me.

Oh, I felt so bad for Mrs. Palmer. She seemed like such a sweet person. More importantly, where was Dean? I wanted to give him my condolences and reassure him that I wasn't involved with Trey. I also wondered about his brothers because there was no sign of them.

I heard footsteps coming back towards the kitchen. "Crystal, this is Officer Jackson." A tall, six-foot man with dark skin came into the kitchen. He smiled and showed his beautiful white teeth—he was very attractive. "

Hello, I'm Rasheed Jackson." He held his hand out towards me. I took his hand and shook it.

"Nice to meet you. I'm Crystal Harris, Dean's colleague," I stated.

"Rasheed is a friend of Dean's from high school," said Mrs. Palmer

"Matter of fact, I saw Dean down the street. He was at the basketball courts. I didn't want to bother him because I figured he was dealing with his dad's passing and I wanted to give him space. I came to pay my respects to you, Aunt Bom Bom,“ Rasheed said.

"I tried to call him earlier, and his phone must be off," Dean's mother said, looking back at Rasheed. "I think Crystal should walk down there."

"I think it is important for me to see him as soon as possible."

"Yes, dear, it is about to storm, hurry down to the corner, and you'll see him. You might be what he needs at this time. Go ahead. It's only at the end of the road.

I got out of my chair and put on my jacket. "Nice to meet you, Rasheed."

Walking down the street toward the basketball court, I was so concerned for Dean. How was he feeling about his father's death? Of course, he would be upset, but in a complex way, considering how cruel his father was towards him. As I got to the park and located the basketball hoops, looking for Dean, my heart dropped, and my mouth opened. My eyes fell on Dean on the left side of the court. He was in an embrace with a woman. A closer look at the short-haired petite woman, and I could tell she was Zara. His ex-girlfriend Zara. I felt like a bowling ball just fallen on my stomach, watching them hold each other. They didn't notice me standing there. My eyes began to water. Tears came down my face. I turned around to go back to the house. I felt like a fool. *I should've never come up here. I'm going to say bye to his mother and head back to Philadelphia.* Walking as fast as I could. I reached the door and noticed that there were more cars at their house; more guests had arrived. I walked up to the door and knocked. Mrs. Palmer opens the door again.

"Crystal, you're back already. Dean's brothers just came back from the florist. You can meet them." She smiled excitedly,

"Sorry, Mrs. Palmer. I have an emergency, and I need to go back to Philly."

"Are you okay, dear? You look upset."

"Yes, I just need to go back to the city. I want you to know it was lovely meeting you, and I wish we could've met under different circumstances."

"Yes, I agree. But what about Dean? Did you get a chance to talk to him?"

"No, I didn't. He was busy with someone else. I'll have to catch up with him later." Tears began to fall from my eyes. "I'll talk to him, but I have to leave now." Hugging Mrs. Palmer and saying goodbye, I walked to my car, opened the door, and started driving. I veered away from the house on a course to return home to the sound of raindrops hitting my windshield. Tears streamed down my face. I drove fast through the puddles, trying to get out of this ridiculous town.

I guess Dean wasn't into me the way I was into him. I feel like a fool

CHAPTER 19
Dean

Feeling exhausted and full of sorrow, I walked into my parents' house. The house was packed with people offering their condolences. Some people were dropping off flowers, offering salads and casseroles. Some people were in the kitchen eating, while others sat having individual conversations, sharing moments of Michael Palmer.

"Dean, I'm so sorry, please accept my condolences," my childhood friend offered before giving me a big hug.

"Hey Rasheed, it's been a long time, man, good to see you, and thank you for coming."

"Yeah, I remember when we were kids, your dad would be at every game, cheering you on. I wish I had a father like yours. He was so dedicated to you. Shoot, I can count on one hand how many times my dad came to my games. He was always working or at the bar with his friends. The community will miss your father."

I wondered how Dad got my friends and the community to believe he was a great father. It seemed that he wasn't as controlling or hard on my two brothers, Hyun-Ki and Cole. They weren't pushed to their limit, just me.

" How are you, son? "

" I'm fine mom, I'm just concerned for you. Is there anything I can do for you? "

"Oh yes, Cole called, and he said they're finishing up the final floral arrangements for the memorial of your father tomorrow," she said, tearing up. "Hey, I called your friend Zara from your job to tell her of the loss of your dad, and she said she's coming here to support us. I know you were an item at one time, but I figured you would want to have your friends at this time."

"Thanks, Mom, for looking out for me. But Zara isn't a friend of mine anymore. I saw her at the courts down the street. She gave me her condolences. Mom, I sent her home. We are not friends, and I don't want fake people around me like her. Mom, please don't tell people I am single, please."

"Dean, what about your other friend from work, did you send her home too?" she said accusingly

"What other friend, Mom?"

"You know, the lady from your company I sent to the courts to see you. That pretty lady with the beautiful smile, Crystal."

"What? Are you saying Crystal was here? How did she know to come here? Where is she?" I asked in confusion.

"Hold on, Dean, with all the questions. First, she showed up here, and I thought she was Zara, and I called her Zara when I opened the door. I welcomed her into the house, and we had tea. We had a good little talk about you and your dad. Then Rasheed came to visit me. Rasheed is a good guy, always looking out for me and asking me to make my special chicken. Anyway, I sent Crystal down to the courts where you and your dad spend so much time together to see you. She went down to see you and came back and said she had an emergency, or she was feeling ill and had to go in a hurry. I tried to get her to stay because the roads are so bad, but she couldn't be convinced."

"Mom, why didn't you tell me right away that Crystal was here? I have to find her. The roads are horrible, and there might be flooding on some of them. I can't believe she was here and she didn't say anything to me!" I said annoyed

The realization came to me. She didn't say anything because my Mom called her Zara, and she must have seen Zara with me at the basketball courts. I hoped she did not see Zara's pathetic attempt to hug me when she put her arms around me and wouldn't let me go. That really pissed me off. She had some nerve showing up here and trying to get back with me. She was nothing to me. Zara wasn't half the woman Crystal was. Crystal was selfless, loyal, and strong, brave, and Zara was a selfish whore.

Mom, I have to go."

"Where are you going, Dean?"

"Mom, I have to find Crystal, she means everything to me."

"What?" she asked, surprised by my words, I was sure.

Kissing mom on the side of the cheek, "Mom, I have to get out of here and find Crystal. Mom, she is the one."

Shocked by my words, she happily shrieked, "The One?"

Looking out the window, "Yes, Mom, The One. My car is blocked in. Tell Rasheed I'm taking his car and his coat. I'll return it later. This is an emergency." I found Rasheed's raincoat and started feeling around for his keys, and when I had them, I ran outside into the heavy rain. I noticed that the wind had picked up more in the past hour. My cell phone kept alerting me to hurricane winds and to find shelter.

Driving on the main roads was almost impossible due to the relentless downpour and high winds. The windshield wipers were going as fast as they could, and visibility was still difficult.

I can't believe Crystal came out here to see me, and I messed it up dealing with Zara. I had to tell her that Zara means nothing to me and never would. *I must find her.* The connection we formed was unlike any other. I felt bad leaving WCP without telling her why I left. Driving faster than I should, I had to find her white BMW X3. After looking on a few routes, I still didn't see her, so I decided to turn the car onto Route 315. When I got onto the turnpike road, there were signs warning of flooding and multiple accidents.

My heart raced thinking something might have happened to Crystal. Driving for about forty minutes on the turnpike, I saw a car in the ravine of the highway with hazard flashers on. As I drove closer, I could see the car was deep in a pool of water and was flooding with water. My heart skipped a beat when I thought of Crystal in the car. I parked on the shoulder and put my hazard and lights on the top of the car so I could be easily seen. I found a flashlight and got out of the car to run to the car. As I got closer to the car, I could identify that it was Crystal's car.

As I got closer, I fell on slick grass into the muddy water that reached up past my waist. The sun was setting, and there was little light to investigate the car with the trees around blocking out the remaining sunlight that was shining through. Looking into the window, I noticed the airbag was deployed, and Crystal was slumped over in her seat belt.

I took a deep breath; I knew a calm head was what was needed. I remembered reading that you never open the car door when a car is in a flood because the pressure will cause more water to go into the car. I took my flashlight and hit the side window. The window didn't break. I slammed the butt of the flashlight over and over until the glass shattered. Reaching deep in the car, I unbuckled the car seat.

"Crystal, Crystal, wake up!!" I yelled at her desperately.

She moaned and moved her head back and forth.

"Oh, thank God, you're alive."

Wrapping my arms under her armpits, I pulled her out with one big thrust. The pressure of pulling her out made my footing slip, and I fell on my back into the Muddy water with Crystal on top of me. Scared for Crystal's safety, I immediately pulled her closer to look at her. She opened her eyes.

"Dean, what are you doing? Why am I on top of you? Wow, you are really wet." Crystal muttered drowsily. Then she closed her eyes and passed out.

Standing up, I put Crystal over my shoulder and walked back to the car through the heavy winds. I opened the back door of the police cruiser and gently laid her down in the back seat.

"I got you, Crystal. I won't ever let anything happen to you. I just need to get you dry and warm."

Closing the door, I got in, hurrying to get us to the nearest shelter. I got off the exit, and next to McDonald's was a Marriott Hotel. Turning off the car lights and pulling in front of the lobby, I ran inside and saw my old basketball buddy. I quickly told him about finding Crystal. He gave me a key to the room and told me not to worry about paying.

I parked and got Crystal in the room. Gently, I laid her in the bed.

Her thick hair cascaded down her face in pretty little curls. She lay on the tan quilt, looking beautiful.

Kissing her cheek, I saw she was shivering. I removed her wet clothes as I dried her body with one of the towels from the bathroom and placed an extra quilt over her in an attempt to get her warm.

"Crystal, I need you to wake up. I need to know you are going to be ok, baby."

I rubbed her goose-bumped arms. Seemed like nothing was working to get her warm. I took off my clothes, leaving my boxers on. I got under the covers and wrapped her around my arms. I wanted the warmth from my body to warm her. I held her tight, occasionally kissing her head and shoulder.

Little moans came from her as she slept. I closed my eyes, loving the way she felt next to my body. Eventually, she stopped shivering, and her teeth stopped chattering.

I knew she was warming up, and her temperature was coming back to normal.

Relieved, I fell asleep with her in my arms.

"Dean, Dean, wake up," I heard Crystal say.

"Hi, baby, how do you feel?"

"I feel fine, just a little tight in my back."

"You had an accident, and I found you on the side of the road. I got you out of the car and took you to the hotel. I am afraid your car has extensive water damage." I said, moving hair out of her face.

"I am sorry that your dad passed away. I went to the basketball court to see you. I saw you with Zara, hugging," Crystal said matter-of-factly.

"You saw her hugging me. My mother invited her, and I had no clue she was coming. You and I were camping, and as you know, we didn't have cell service. I was at the hoops trying to have a moment to myself, and Zara stopped me. She came to me before she went to see my mother. She said she wanted to be here for me during my time of need. She then hugged me. I did NOT reciprocate the hug. Think, Crystal, about what you saw. You saw her arms on me. Not my arms around her."

"I guess you're right. I didn't take the time to take in the scene. Where is she now? Is she at your mother's home?"

"No, she isn't. I sent her home when I was at the courts. She's not a friend of mine. I only want people who care about my family and me here. I don't have time for fake people," I said, bending down to kiss her forehead.

"Oh, you sent her home? You were serious about not liking her."

"Yes, I am not fake. She is someone I prefer never to be around. What I want to know is what made you come to see me? How did you find out about my dad?"

"I tried to contact you, but you weren't answering my texts or calls. I figured you were upset with me."

"Why would I be upset with you?"

"Well, first, JP gave me the position."

"Oh yeah, congratulations. I am so happy for you, Crystal. You deserve it. I wanted to congratulate you, but I just heard from my family about my dad. JP gave me the news first thing in the morning. He offered me the Senior Executive of Strategic Sales position. I accepted the position."

"That is terrific, I didn't know the Senior Executive of Strategic Sales was open. This is great news. You and I both will be on the 6th floor."

She lifted her head to give me a kiss.

"The other reason I came to see you was that I saw you look at me after I gave a man a long hug at the office. I wanted to explain it to you. I didn't want you to think I had a man."

I started laughing. "I wasn't concerned with you hugging Trevon or Trey, some call him, that's my boy."

"What? You know him?"

"We play ball together, and he's my massage therapist. He is a great guy. There isn't a slimy bone in his body. He helped a lot with the Zara breakup."

"Oh wow. I am so happy to hear you know Trey! I guess I was concerned for no reason." Crystal said, clearly relieved.

"Crys, you're the only girl for me. I don't want to spend a day without seeing you. I'm so happy you're here with me. I would usually deal with issues alone. But I trust you, and I want you by my side during this time. I have so many mixed emotions when it comes to my father..."

"I can only imagine. Dean, as long as I'm around, you will never be alone. I've got your back, just like you have mine."

Crystal

We kissed, and since we both had all our clothes off, we took advantage of the hotel. Dean began kissing my shoulder and the back of my neck. His hands grabbed my left breast. I purred with delight at his touch. Something about this man and the way he touches me, my body goes haywire. He started to kiss down my spine. Then he went to my breast and began massaging in a circular motion. I could feel my lady parts respond instantly.

"Oh, Dean, you feel so good," I moaned.

He moved his hand to my butt, and he caressed each cheek. His trail of kisses went down my back and settled on my ass. He cupped each cheek and kissed and gently bit, enjoying all this ass. After he was done playing with my ass, he turned me on my back.

"I want you to relax and enjoy it while I feast," Dean said seductively,

pulling my legs apart. He placed his body between my legs, bent my left leg up and moved it wider.

"You are so beautiful down here, Crystal." He put his tongue to my love button and then inside me. He came up and kissed me, trailing my stomach through the canyon between my breasts. I could feel him sizing his member to my opening. I could feel him slowly and persistently pushing his way into me. I was very much inviting the pleasure of him inside me. I moaned in ecstasy at his first thrust. He continued to move rhythmically and lovingly. He was trying to make sure he did not hurt me. I appreciated his caring, loving way, but I could handle more.

"Dean, I am not going to break, I am not a China doll. I am ok, be yourself. I want you to be the way you would if you were not concerned with me being in the accident."

Dean showed he understood by nodding. Well, he must have fully comprehended. He immediately began moving faster and deeper. I immediately inhaled and kept inhaling in efforts to keep up with him. He was silent, other than taking deep breaths. He was working this pussy. He had a job, and he was not going to lose focus; he understood the assignment. I felt his hand go down my leg as he continued to work my pussy. He took my leg and placed it on his shoulder. He felt so deep. I had to take a deep breath to handle his long, thick length. I could feel my pussy adjusting to handle all that length and width. It took me a few seconds to get used to the deep vigor he was giving me. I was on the verge to climaxing. Dean took my other leg and placed it on his shoulder. Now both legs were on his shoulders, and he was not letting up, he was strong and deep. I gave up trying to keep up with his rhythm. This was his pussy, and I allowed him to control, as he drove me to ecstasy. There was no way I could keep up. He was like in a trance; he was not letting up. His two hands went under my ass cheeks and lifted my ass for better access to me. This was the most intense.

At this point, I was moaning and yelling. Dean began to speak Korean in a deep, harsh voice. I couldn't understand a word he was saying, but I knew it was something good because his face showed he was in delight. He said something in Korean again. He sped up, and I couldn't take it- I climaxed and cried out loud. He yelled a Korean word louder and said I love you in English. Then he climaxed. We held each other, shaking and loving each other. He stayed inside me until we collapsed in exhaustion.

We lay there looking at each other and rubbing and stroking each other's backs and shoulders.

" You ok, Crys?" he whispered

"Yes, I am good, Dean, I am great," I said, satisfied.

"I mean what I said, Crystal. I love you, and I am in love with you," he revealed.

When he said he loved me, a jolt of electricity ran through me, and I could feel my kitty throbbing for more.

"Dean, babe, I feel the same. I am in love with you." We kissed some more. "Dean, I have a question. What did you say in Korean? I didn't know you could speak Korean."

"Well, I can tell you, or I can show you," Dean said seductively.

We both laughed, hugged, and kissed until we fell asleep.

This man, my hero. I giggled with glee.

Epilogue

It has been one year since Dean confessed his love to me, and I confessed my feelings to him as well. I will never forget how Dean, aka My Hero, saved me from my accident. I think that was the turning point in our relationship. When we were in the woods camping, we got a chance to get to know each other better. I kept admiring his strong shoulders and back as he worked on the campsite. I noticed him stealing glances of me when he thought I was busy. We stopped resisting our attraction and surrendered to our desire; nevertheless, we discovered that we have more in common than we had imagined.

We both got over the old hangups that we got from our old, failed relationships. I was happy to admit that I have stopped dreaming about Spencer and thinking that any man who showed interest in me might play with my emotions. A friend in WCP London told me the gossip in the office is that Spencer was miserable, and he had been keeping up with the progress of my career.

I thought that was hilarious.

Dean has moved on as well. He's no longer guarded and now more trusting of me, recognizing I'm not like his ex, Zara. He understands every woman is unique and not all will hurt him. Plus, a few weeks ago, we heard Zara got fired because of poor performance. Sophia heard that she was dating her married boss. The wife found out her husband was cheating. She demanded that Zara leave the company and the relationship come to an end. So, she had to go. Zara has not been seen since her discharge.

Dean and I had become completely inseparable. Our bond has grown so strong that we find ourselves wanting to spend every moment together. I truly love the way our relationship has evolved.

Tonight, we have a big celebration to attend for the product Dean and I worked on, Dermacore. I know we will be recognized at the product launch party, so I wanted to make sure I look good. I consulted Davi, my new stylist, and she assured me this outfit will be a hit. She selected an off-the-shoulder cream colored fitted dress that was above the knee, accompanied by the most beautiful shoes. I slid on two-inch crystal-studded, Jimmy Choo sling-back pumps. The shoes were perfect as they sparkle.

Dean was coming to pick up Mom and me. We were getting ready, so we were ready to leave when he came to pick us up.

"Mom, are you just about ready?"

My mother walked into the living room in a navy blue colored satin dress with a soft, draped neckline. Her hair was freshly dyed red, curled tight, and pinned up with a side-swept bang. She looked so elegant; it had been ages since I'd seen her look this classy. Watching her, I couldn't help but feel something shift inside me. She looked like the mom I knew when I was younger, before she got depressed and secluded herself to the couch watching her television.

"Crystal, how do I look? "Mom sang, twirling her dress so I could get a good look.

"You look beautiful, Mom. The dress fits you beautifully. Your makeup and hair style make you look glamorous.

Kissing me on the cheek, mom replied," Thank you, Crystal Sweetie. You are as pretty as a picture. Dean will not be able to keep his eyes off you. You know honey, I am so proud of you. You are one of the strongest women I know. You found happiness and peace because you are strong and brave. Watching you over the years, overcome breakups and make a strong name for yourself at WCP. You also did not allow heartbreak to break you. It has made me think about the way I have lived my life. I am going to make some changes starting today. No longer will I occupy my time in front of the television. I need to get out and meet people. I need to get a life. Next Thursday is bingo night, I will be going there to have a good time and hopefully make some new acquaintances".

With tears about to pour out of my eyes and ruin my makeup, I cried. "Oh, Mom, I love you so much. I have been waiting for you to say those words." We hugged and cried happy tears.

At that moment, the doorbell rang.

"Come in, Dean," I yelled toward the door.

Dean entered the house, and his eyes fell on me. A bright smile appeared on his handsome face. He wore a tapered slate blue suit. The cut complicated him perfectly, the fabric skimming the broad line of his shoulders and tapering sharply at his waist. A crisp white shirt and the champagne tie set the outfit off.

"How are my two favorite ladies? You both look stunning," as he placed a kiss on each of our cheeks.

"Dean, Crystal, and I are ready to go to the celebration. I want you both to know I am so proud of both of you. I couldn't think of a better man to have in my daughter's life.

"Aww, Mom, that is so sweet," I said.

"Thank you, Ms. Harris. My life is better because I have Crystal to share my it with. I thank you for raising a daughter I admire and love. Now, you two take an arm and let's go to the WCP Ball, I mean celebration," Dean said.

We arrived at the WCP celebration for Dermacore Product at the Rittenhouse Hotel, where the room was decorated with white and blue flowers and cocktail tables featuring the new logo. Catering by famous Chef Shawn Warely. Jazz music played as guests gathered near a stage with a balloon arch displaying the Dermacore logo. All Philadelphia branch employees attended, including Liam Russell and his team, Brian, Sophia, with Lady Sugar in tow, JP and his two uncles, Dean's family, and my close friends Mabel, Lelia, and Chaundra.

Whispering in Dean's ear, "This room is beautiful. I think JP is going to give a speech soon."

"Yes, Crystal, I think we made it just in time," he whispered back.

JP got on stage and thanked the hard-working scientist on the product. He explained the purpose of Dermacore and how it will change the way people interact with each other. JP made sure to give Liam Russell his acknowledgement by inviting him on stage to give a speech. Liam respectfully declined the opportunity. JP then called for Dean and me to come to the stage.

JP says, "All of this could not be possible if it wasn't for these two people, Crystal Harris and Dean Palmer. They worked on the product partnership to create Dermacore, a co-branding. Would you like to say something, Crystal, Dean?

"I would like to say, Thank you to the team. This is the beginning of a shared legacy. We are two companies that have different backgrounds but are united with the same purpose. I am very excited and proud to be part of the product. Thank you, Dean. Would you like to say something?

Dean took the microphone, "Thank you, Ms. Harris. I would like to add. As many of you know, Crystal and I started out as rivals, and our mission was to make the joint venture between the companies become a success. With the help of JP's special assignment, we learned to work together. We have a newfound appreciation for each other's talents. I can say that this product has brought us together. Dean turns towards me and stops addressing the audience.

"Crystal, our hearts were on two different courses and we found each other. You are my everything and more."

What was Dean doing? Why was Dean talking about our relationship to me? He was not being professional. I wonder if I should stop him from going further.

"I admire your wit, strength, beauty, fearlessness, and your sharp tongue," he laughed.

Dean continued, "There is no other woman I want to spend my days and nights with. Crystal, I want you to be my wife. Will you marry me?"

As Dean spoke, he dropped to one knee and presented a box containing an impressively large diamond ring. Dean was proposing to me, asking me to marry him. Completely stunned, I simply stared at him for a moment.

"Crystal, did you hear me? Will you marry me?" he asked louder.

I gazed down at him and said, " Yes, Dean, yes, I will marry you."

The room erupted into applause. Dean stood up, slipped the four-carat princess-cut ring onto my finger, and we kissed while the audience shouted and cheered for us.

In the audience, we heard a scream, " No...No.No!" come from the crowd. The room parted to reveal Zara screaming, " No Dean, you can't get married, I still love you. You know we are meant to be with each other."

Dean and I stood there in shock, and the room was silent.

Sophia walked toward Zara, broke the silence as she exclaimed, "Oh no, Zara, you will not do this to Dean and Crystal. I had enough of you. You need to leave, and I will assist you." Sophia grabbed her arm and escorted her out the doors, with Lady Sugar following.

As the doors closed, the crowd cheered in delight.

My attention went to Dean, "I love you, babe. You really surprised me by asking me to marry you at the launch. I can't believe we are engaged. Who else was in on this proposal scheme?"

Dean chuckled and smiled, "Sweetie, I wanted to make sure it surprised you. I wanted to have our coworkers, friends, and family present. Sorry, babe, all your friends and family knew I was going to pop the question. I needed to talk to your friends and family to get them to help me to pick out the ring. Do you like the ring, babe?'

"Yes, I adore it, and I adore you, Dean. I'm still in disbelief," I said dreamily. "I can't wait for us to begin our next chapter together."

With all the hurdles Dean and I went through, I know he was the right man for me. He closed his heart off for so long. The fact that he professed his love to me in front of friends, family, and coworkers. He was serious about us. I was proud of myself. Once, I had said all men were not to be trusted. I trusted Dean with my whole heart. Being with him just feels right. What I couldn't believe was that his ex-girlfriend stepped in to mess up our engagement. Where did she get off? I hoped she wasn't a problem for us in the future, because I had no problem putting Miss Zara in her place.

I noticed Sophia coming back into the room after handling Zara. I really love Sophia; she really had my back. I saw Sophia return to the room with her dog Lady Sugar. Sophia announces to the room, "It is all good, folks. I took out the trash, and trust me, she won't be returning." The crowd erupted with laughter.

I noticed Mr. Russell walk over to Sophia and say, "Ms. Sophia, I like the way you work, you are very impressive. I have a proposition for you, I think you may be interested in. May I call you tomorrow? "Liam said seductively.

Sophia smiled softly at Liam, nodding slowly while keeping her gaze fixed on him. She understood she was agreeing to more than just mere words.

The jazz music ended, Alicia Keys' "If I Ain't Got You" played, and a spotlight illuminated us as the lights dimmed.

Dean said, "Crystal, come dance with me?"

I gave Dean my hand as he led me to the floor. We slow danced while everyone watched us.

"Crystal, you realize this is our engagement party, we have all our loved ones here. We have a DJ, food, and a photographer. From the first time I saw your sexy ass, I knew it was something about you I couldn't get out of my head and eventually out of my heart. You know I would like to have a short engagement," Dean whispered in my ear as we swayed back and forth.

"Why a short engagement, Dean?"

"Because Crystal, I don't want to waste any time starting our lives together. Too much time was wasted on us not being happy. You make me happy, and I can't wait to come home and lay my eyes on you every day.

"I love you, babe. I am fine with a short engagement. I have a great idea. Let's go camping for our honeymoon... just kidding, Dean, ," I giggled

We both laughed and kissed each other for a very, very inappropriately long time.

Until our wedding.

Jason Pfeiffer

Bonus Chapter

I met my twin uncles, Hedrick and Kendrick Pfieffer, in the back room of the venue. They were eccentric but successful executives at WCP Industries. Hendrick is the CEO and founder of the company. They were my favorite uncles growing up, thanks to their constant pranks, which some relatives found annoying, but I always enjoyed. Now adults, their pranks had become more elaborate, often involving matchmaking schemes with unsuspecting employees. I knew it wasn't Human Resources approved, but they have not been found out yet.

"Hi, Uncle Kendrick, Uncle Hendrick, thank you for coming to the launch party and engagement party. It has been a while since we were all together."

Both uncles gave me a hug.

"How did I do with the continuation of the tradition uncles? I was surprised by how enjoyable it was to see everything unfold," I said proudly.

Uncle Hendrick sparkled with pride as he turned toward me.

"I am so impressed," he said, his voice full of enthusiasm. "You did a fantastic job matchmaking Crystal and Dean. They never knew you set them up." He smiled, pleased with the outcome.

"I am so happy you enjoyed it. There is nothing quite like the rush of getting two people in those uncomfortable situations and watching them squirm. Eventually they will have to give in to discomfort. The real question is, will they end up falling in love or will they hate each other?" Uncle Hendrick let out a loud giggle, clearly relishing the suspense and excitement that came with every match he orchestrated.

Uncle Kendrick laughed heartily, "I can say it is my favorite pastime. Sometimes you up the matchmaking when they get a little help with the right cocktail, if you know what I mean," he said with a mischievous grin.

Uncle Hendrick and I both frowned at Uncle Kendrick's comment.

"No, I think that is going too far, Uncle, no special cocktails should be used. That is cheating and creepy. You have always gone a little too far outside the lines, Uncle," I said, reprimanding him.

"Ok, you're right. I am going too far. But maybe the next matchmaking will be *you,* nephew. You are getting older, and I never see you with a girlfriend. Do you need help? Because you know we're experts at this matchmaking game," Kendrick said confidently with a big grin.

"Oh no, no, I do not need any help. No, thank you. I don't need or want help from either of you," I said, laughing as we walked back to the party.

Every ending is just a new beginning in disguise.

THE END.

www.ingramcontent.com/pod-product-compliance
Lightning Source LLC
La Vergne TN
LVHW090524110826
845146LV00003B/974

* 9 7 9 8 9 9 3 6 1 5 5 1 6 *